THARAEN

Immortal Highlander Book 2

HAZEL HUNTER

ALLURE PRESS

HH ONLINE

Hazel loves hearing from readers!
You can contact her at the links below.

Website: hazelhunter.com

Facebook:
business.facebook.com/HazelHunterAuthor

Newsletter: HazelHunter.com/news

I send newsletters with details on new releases,
special offers, and other bits of news related to my
writing. You can sign up here!

Chapter One

✿❦✿

BEING WELL OVER six feet tall had its advantages, though not as many when you were a woman. Lieutenant Diana Burke stood up to stretch her long limbs, and saw the rest of the gray cubicles around her had already emptied. One advantage of being well over six feet tall was the ability to check her surroundings in a few seconds. Beyond the maze of sound-reducing panels, the building's glass exterior panels showed the glitter of harbor lights against a matte black sky. The last time she'd looked, the view had been of the city's skyscrapers, framed by a silver-blue sky slashed with gold-edged clouds.

Inside her right temple she felt the warning

tap of another headache, and reached for the pill bottle in her top drawer.

Down in the Gaslamp Quarter the party would just be getting started. She hadn't gone there to drink at her favorite rooftop bar since she'd started putting in the extra hours that she didn't report on her time sheet. The hours were hers, and she'd do what she wanted with them. Wasting them on frozen strawberry margaritas and guys who blanched the minute she stood up didn't appeal much to her anymore.

But finding the lost, and bringing them home, made every damn day Christmas morning.

The smell of vanilla made Diana frown, until she saw the slice of cake someone had left parked on the end of her desk. That meant a birthday today in the unit, and she'd missed it. It annoyed her. She really liked the people she worked with, and she loved cake of any kind.

Except red velvet. Even thinking about it made her shudder a little. Why would anyone like cake the color of blood? It was almost as bad as those decorated sugar skulls and skeletons they sold around the city for *Dia de los Muertos*.

Being the last one to leave work didn't bother Diana. Most of the cops assigned to the Missing

Persons Unit at the San Diego Police Department worked overtime without pay whenever a child or an endangered adult went missing, but it had been a quiet week. Only fifteen new reports, all on adults who were not considered at risk, had been filed. They also hadn't had an AMBER alert all month. Typically ninety-nine percent of missing adults would be found within forty-eight hours, usually in good health. A few would take longer to return home, but eventually they'd show.

One percent, however, would never come back. If MPU was very lucky, in a few years a hunter or hiker would find what was left. Covering those crime scenes was probably what had rendered Diana incapable of eating candy bones on the Day of the Dead. She saw too much of the real deal.

Knowing food would help keep the headache pills from burning in her gut, Diana scooped up and ate the cake with one hand while she used the other to outbox the stack of reports she'd finally finished. The paperwork was her least favorite part of the job, but tomorrow afternoon she'd do it again. It had become part of her new daily routine since her last partner had transferred over to the Sheriff's Department. Updating all the case files had fallen in Diana's lap, along with all the other work she used to share. She'd be flying solo for another month until her new partner finished forensic imaging training.

That was something else she needed to add to the running list in her head: *Be here for the newbie to go over the files and bring him or her up to speed. Right after I find Kinley and decide what to do with Baby.*

The cake only made Diana feel hungrier, so she strolled over to steal some jelly beans from the unit secretary's desk jar as she checked the hall. The janitor's cart sat two doors down, and a couple of uniforms stood at the far end talking to the nightshift desk sergeant. When they spotted her they lifted hands in hello, and she did the same. The taller of the two uniforms had the pressed-but-clueless look of a recent academy graduate. He gave her the once-over and widened his grin.

"Oh, don't even tempt me, rook," Diana muttered as she retreated back into the office to grab her things. "I'd snap you like cheap china."

What she needed was to go home, throw together a reasonably healthy stir-fry, soak in the tub, and go to bed before three a.m. The phone on her desk rang, suggesting that she wouldn't.

"MPU, Lieutenant Burke," she said as she tucked the phone receiver between her cheek and shoulder to shrug into her blazer.

"It's Gerry Stevens," the psychiatrist said, sounding apologetic. "I thought I'd touch base with you one more time before I fly up to Seattle tomorrow. I've been transferred."

"Sorry to hear that," Diana said. She knew Dr. Stevens had been fighting to stay at San Diego's VA hospital ever since her patient's baffling disappearance, in which she may or may not have played a part. Diana felt pretty sure it was a not. "Nothing new to report, I'm afraid. We haven't had any calls on the tip line in months, and there's been zero activity on her credit cards and bank accounts." She didn't mention that Captain Kinley Chandler's missing persons' file had been officially moved to cold cases, or that she'd unofficially made a copy of it and was still investigating.

A tired sigh came over the line. "I don't know why I can't let this go. It's been a year since Kinley vanished. She couldn't walk, and without medical treatment... Do you think she's dead, Diana? She has to be."

"Until we find a body," Diana said, "we don't

give up hope." She grabbed her keys from her desk drawer, and then made a promise she would probably break. "I'm going to keep looking for her, Gerry, and we'll keep in touch. Give me a call once you're settled."

"Okay," the psychiatrist said. "Thank you, for everything."

Diana replaced the receiver and watched the line light blink off. She usually didn't get on a first-name basis with civilians, but Geraldine Stevens had been calling her twice a week for the last year. She'd also met her at the crime scene, and walked and talked the detective through every moment she'd spent there with Kinley Chandler before the captain had vanished. That Gerry blamed herself for it was a given. She'd taken the badly-injured captain from her VA hospital to Horsethief Canyon, reportedly as a therapeutic outing. From all the reports the psychiatrist had provided, the captain had been seriously depressed, and possibly suicidal.

Only there was no blood, no signs of trauma or a struggle, and no body. The only evidence forensics had found was Chandler's wheelchair, sitting empty on the trail. They hadn't even found any footprints in the soil around it.

After a year of working the case Diana knew just about everything there was to know about Chandler. She'd read her entire medical chart, her service record and the incident reports about the insurgent attack that had nearly killed her in Afghanistan. She knew she drank her coffee black, voted independent, cut her own hair, and splurged on a pricey gardenia body wash that smelled pretty heavenly. Diana had even read some of the biographies and history books about Scotland she'd found in Kinley's house. While the facts pointed to an abduction, possibly to facilitate the captain's suicide, all of Diana's instincts told her otherwise. Unlike Geraldine Stevens, she had no emotional connection to the victim, so it wasn't wishful thinking.

Whether or not a third party had helped her, or abducted her, or beamed her up out of that wheelchair to their alien mothership, somewhere out there Kinley Chandler was still alive. Diana didn't just feel it. She *knew* it—just as she had known about her mother.

Her gaze shifted to the only personal item on her desk, a framed photograph of herself in a cap and gown, and a short, heavyset Italian man in a badly-fitting brown suit.

Her friendship with Detective Tonio Leoni had begun when he'd visited her at the hospital. After learning why she'd been admitted, he'd helped her case worker move her to a new group home run by church people. He'd also appointed himself her unofficial mentor, checking on her with weekly phone calls and monthly visits. He'd never threatened her or talked down to her, and when she got fresh with him he'd only chuckle.

"Kid, I work Vice," he'd told her after she'd sworn at him once. "You're going to have to come up with something better than 'nosy fat bastard' to curl my hair."

She hadn't realized it at the time, but Tonio had probably saved her life. Even if she had managed to survive her health situation, teen runaways usually came to bad ends. If they didn't wind up as drug addicts who sold themselves until they overdosed, they were murdered or committed suicide. Keeping her from becoming another wretched statistic wasn't the cop's only motive for taking an interest.

"I've kept tabs on you for eight years," he'd told her when she'd asked why he'd come to see her at the hospital. "Ever since your mom left you at the station. I was on duty that night, and I knew your mother. But you, you kept telling me that you could show me where she was."

She was tempted to tell him about the weird feeling she got in her chest when she looked for lost things—or how she almost always found them. But she didn't trust grownups, and he probably wouldn't believe her anyway.

"Didn't anyone go and look for her?" Diana demanded.

"Yeah. I did." His mouth flattened. "And you were right. I found her a week later, exactly where you said she'd be."

She knew why he didn't want to tell her any more than that. "How did she die?"

Tonio took her hand in his, and sighed. "Bunch of sleeping pills mixed with booze. She was just a kid herself, got pregnant in school, and ran away from home. But she made sure you'd be safe before she did herself in, Di. You remember that she cared enough to do that first."

It took Diana a few more years to realize that Tonio had known her mother because he worked Vice, and she'd been a prostitute.

Knowing the truth hurt, but it also freed Diana from the useless dreams every foster kid had of being reclaimed by their real family. From that day she'd known she was on her own for good. The only life she would have would be one she made for herself. Tonio had helped, first by getting her through high school, and then by finding enough scholarship money to put her through college. She'd come out with a criminal justice degree, and applied to the academy. Tonio had been the one to present her with her badge when she'd graduated.

"Look for the lost ones, kid," he'd told her when she'd asked how she could ever repay him for being her mentor. "You save one, you save the world."

"I'm going to find her, Tonio," Diana said as she touched the edge of the photo. Her mentor had died suddenly three years ago of a heart attack, but she always felt as if he was still watching over her.

As Diana left headquarters she pulled on her Padres ball cap, and strolled to the far end of the lot, where she always parked Baby, her '51 Cadillac convertible. The black and chrome monster looked like a dinosaur, especially these days with everyone in the city driving electric cars and hybrids. Diana didn't care. Her Baby was her one, self-indulgent bit of heaven on earth. She'd bought it as a rusty old hulk from a scrap yard when she was twenty, and spent every spare dime she had getting it completely restored. She loved every inch of it, from the wide white-wall tires to the mirror finish on the battering ram bumpers.

Hell, if she had her way she'd be buried in it, but Baby deserved better.

Diana climbed in and eyed herself in the rearview mirror. She'd never be beautiful, not with her angular face and bold features, but lately she'd let herself get a bit ragged. Dark circles showed through her faded concealer to raccoon her pale violet eyes. When she was brooding she dragged the edge of her teeth back and forth over her lower lip, which now looked as raw as it felt. She had to start eating better, too. The gaunt hollows in her cheeks and throat were becoming more noticeable again.

Without warning a huge wave of fatigue crashed over her, churning her stomach and sending the shakes through her limbs. She sat back and let it happen, closing her eyes as she endured the familiar nausea and fear. It felt like being pulled under by a rip current. The more she fought it, the deeper she sank. Diana recalled the image of the missing Air Force captain, and focused on that until the exhaustion and need to puke receded.

"No," she muttered and pushed some short spikes of her scanty red hair up under her ball cap, settling it more firmly on her head before she started the powerful engine. "Not until I find Kinley."

Driving past the road to her apartment made Diana feel better. So did stopping at her favorite drive-through for a big vanilla milk shake and three orders of fries to fill her growling stomach.

"Hey, Detective," Jake said, as the grinning blond kid at the window handed out her order. He'd been serving her hot, salty fries several times a week since she'd gotten the Chandler case. "Find Waldo yet?"

She gave him the official cop scowl. "Why? You know where he is?"

They both laughed at the very lame joke, and she handed him back a fiver out of her change.

"What's this for?" Jake demanded.

"The college fund," Diana said, shaking a long fry at him. "Stanford, guy. I'm counting on you getting in."

He laughed. "More like Mesa, if I don't fail

calculus again. By the way, no one says *guy* anymore."

She shrugged. "I call you bro, you might try to borrow some serious money from me."

"Like you'd have any." He rolled his bright blue eyes. "Watch the road, Detective."

As she headed up the interstate toward Horsethief Canyon, Diana talked out her ideas on the case. She'd gone over the details a million times, but it helped. She never knew when she'd hit on a new angle.

"Okay, so Blondie's combat search and rescue. She knows how to get in and out of tight spots. Maybe she already has a phone on her when she sends Geraldine back to the van to get hers. She makes the call to whoever followed them to the canyon. 'Come get me,' says Kinley." Diana ate the fry she was holding and took another from the carton. "Military pal comes in, grabs her, erases his footprints with a branch, and hikes out through the canyon with her to another vehicle, which he uses to transport her to…where?"

The fry didn't answer, but it tasted delicious.

"Doesn't make sense," Diana told the rearview mirror as she checked it. "If Blondie wanted to die, she was doing a pretty good job of it at the hospital. Not fast enough, maybe? Or she had stuff to do before the final deed? What stuff? No living family, no friends stateside, and no boyfriend. No one to take her out of there. Gerry wanted her to live. That puts us back to square one."

Diana took the exit for the canyon. As she passed the fire station she considered who else Kinley might have convinced to transport her. She had interviewed every single member of the hospital staff who had come in contact with Kinley. Each and every one of them had solid alibis for their whereabouts during the time of the disappearance. She'd even met with the captain's previous shrink, a skinny, stuffy jackass named Patterson, who had tried to patronize her and had ended up on the defensive.

"Kinley Chandler had no interest in her own recovery," the psychiatrist told her, pressing his bony fingers to his temple as if he felt a migraine coming on. "She didn't socialize, she stopped eating, and she slept twenty hours a day. I believe she had survivor's guilt, and diagnosed her as high risk for suicide."

"But she never attempted to kill herself while under your care," Diana pointed out. "And she refused the pain meds which she could have squirreled away to do the deed. When I checked her hospital room, I saw about twenty things she might have used to kill herself. Active duty combat —they're trained to be resourceful."

"Being at risk for suicide is not the same thing as committing it," Patterson told her. "Chandler was clearly building up to the act in an opportunity-restricted environment. Now if you'll excuse me, I have a patient waiting."

Later Diana had asked Gerry Stevens if Patterson might have helped Kinley get out of the canyon. The psychiatrist suggested only if he'd been held at gunpoint.

Once Diana parked her Caddy in the lot by the canyon trail, she finished her fries and milkshake, and deposited her trash in the park can before fetching her big flashlight from the trunk. She paused for a moment to clear her head with her personal mantra: *Save one, save the world.*

"All right, Blondie," Diana said as she switched on the high-powered light. "Let's see if we can find out something new tonight."

⚜

LITTLE NOISES RUSTLED on either side of the trail as Diana made her way up to the crime scene, but nothing jumped out to bite her. She kept her hand on the Glock 19 in her hip holster, just in case something got braver. Diana was fine with nature, as long as it kept its poisonous fangs away from her ankles.

At the oak grove, one lonely strip of faded yellow crime scene tape fluttered in the breeze. Every time she came to the spot she noticed first how quiet it was, as if nothing but the wind and the oak leaves were allowed to be heard. It also felt a little cooler than every other spot in the canyon, but she attributed that to the density of the tree canopy. Her own imagination probably factored in, as it was here that a battered, dying woman had spent her last moments before seemingly evaporating into thin air.

"Hey, Kinley," Diana said. She always talked to her victim when she was alone at the scene. "It's your favorite cop again. Miss me?" She walked around a bit, breathing in the cool night air. "I know. I should have come by this weekend, when I'd have daylight to help me. Can't wait for it." She turned from side to side, using the light to sweep the grove. "Come on, Blondie. We're running out of time. Give me something."

Diana walked a full circle of the scene, aiming the flashlight on the soil and the trees. The ruts left by Kinley's wheelchair had long ago been scoured away by the wind, although she did notice some new root growth from the oaks showing through fresh breaks in the topsoil.

"I'm guessing you guys are older than dirt, so good for you." She crouched down to touch the knobs of one root, and snatched her hand back. She rubbed her tingling fingertips, dropping the flashlight in the process. "Damn it! This better not be poison ivy."

She held her hand in the light to check her skin, and then looked up.

The beam of light shone across the grove to a gap that Diana had never before noticed. Slowly she picked up the flashlight and moved it over the area until she realized what it was.

"That's the edge of that dried-up waterfall," she murmured. When she stood she couldn't see it anymore. She dropped back down, positioning herself as if she were sitting in a wheelchair, and clearly saw the gap again. "Son of a bitch. Could you have made that on your own?" It wasn't that

far, maybe a dozen steps. Her heart clenched as
she straightened. "Aw, Blondie. Tell me you didn't
jump and get your wrecked ass stuck in some
rocks on the way down."

Diana started to take a step toward the gap,
and then hesitated. If her victim had leapt to her
death, and her body had gotten wedged before
hitting the ground, the critters in the canyon still
would have disposed of her remains. Even bones
would be scattered by now. She probably wasn't
going to see anything when she looked over the
edge but darkness, and she had enough of that in
her head.

Until we find a body, we don't give up hope.

"Damn it," Diana said. "I can't believe you
took a dive. I know it was bad, you were a mess
and in terrible pain and about to lose your leg, but
what the hell, Blondie?" She threw out her arms.
"You survived Afghanistan to do *this*? Do you
know how it's going to screw with Gerry when she
finds out? Your shrink is one bad phone call away
from a breakdown."

Maybe Diana would forget about what she'd
seen and walk away. She could stick her notes in
the cold case file and forget about Captain Kinley

Chandler. The next cop who dug into it could look over the edge.

Only she couldn't walk away. She'd been carrying Kinley's sad, heartbreaking image in her head for twelve months now. If there was anything left of her to bury, Diana needed to know. Then she could close this case, solve the biggest mystery of her career and, when the time came, go out a winner.

Looking up at the night sky cleared Diana's head. "Right. Quit whining and do the job." She started toward the gap, caught the edge of her boot on a root and went down hard.

Her knees slammed into nothing as the flashlight skittered out of her hand. Diana fell straight down into a dark, whirling tunnel of threshing leaves and branches and tree trunks. She couldn't get out a scream, but she clamped her palm on her Glock. No light, no end, and as she fell deeper and faster she knew when she hit the bottom of whatever sinkhole she'd fallen into she was going to be smashed to smithereens.

Oddly that thought comforted her. No better way to go out than instantaneously—and maybe that was why Kinley had thrown herself over the edge.

Chapter Two

✦❧✦

DIANA'S DROP SEEMED to slow as the trees crowded around her, and then spread back out. She finally hit bottom, only it wasn't bottom. She was back on the ground, and outside, but the sky was golden, not black, and the sun was only just setting. The trees around her looked different—smaller, and somehow older—and beyond them rose some pretty impressive mountains. Weathered slabs of odd-looking rock, half-buried in the ground, formed an irregular ring around her. The air she dragged in made her lungs tingle from the cold crispness. Somewhere close by the sound of water rushed, and then birds were singing.

Slowly she pushed herself up to see a huge, furry red deer with a gray face staring at her.

"Ah, hi there, Nature."

The deer let out something that sounded like a high-pitched, extra-long burp, and took off. Diana covered her head and cringed as an entire herd of deer jumped over her and around her as they followed.

Once the wildlife left the building it took another couple of minutes for Diana to stand and test her legs. Her bum knee, which should have been throbbing up a storm, felt great. Better than great. It felt like it had been replaced with a titanium knee that would never wear out. Adrenalin did wonders for the shocked as shit, Diana decided as she holstered her weapon. She turned around to scope out her surroundings.

That was when she saw that she wasn't in California anymore.

The sea was different, and on the wrong side of her. She also knew it couldn't be seen from a place as far inland as Horsethief Canyon. She added the grass, the thick carpet of feathery ferns, and trumpet-shaped blue flowers to her wrong list. No chaparral anywhere, only oak trees. Lots and lots of oak trees.

Diana heard a rustle and drew her weapon. "Step out and show yourselves, now."

The man and woman who shuffled out into the open looked at her with the same confusion she felt. Both were dressed in crudely-sewn tunics, belted shawls and wore funny caps on their heads. From their stained, handmade leather boots to their bad haircuts, everything about them shouted serious cosplay.

"Hi," Diana said. She took out her badge and showed it to them. "Lieutenant Burke, San Diego Police. Would you mind telling me where I am?"

The woman tried to muffle a shriek with her hand. The man didn't bother trying. They both took off the same way the deer had gone.

"Thank you for your cooperation," she said quietly, replacing her badge.

As good as her knee felt, Diana considered chasing after them. But a strange glimmer caught her eye. At first it looked like someone had left a trail of golden glitter through the grass, but as she drew closer she saw the sparkles were actual light, floating just above the ground. When she knelt down to touch the substance, it wound around her fingers, glowing even brighter. It disappeared as soon as she lifted her hand away from the rest of the trail, leaving behind a whiff of something like very pricey gardenia-scented soap.

Crap.

She stood. Jake wouldn't have spiked her milk-shake with drugs. Diana would swear to that. He was a good kid who genuinely liked her. She wasn't hallucinating, either. She'd done plenty of that, and it didn't feel like this. This felt real, and there was another thing that freaked her out a little.

The sparkles felt like Captain Kinley Chandler. Hell, they even smelled like her.

The trail of golden light tugged at Diana, and so did something else. It seemed to be reaching into her chest and grabbing at her heart. She looked up at the jagged ridges of the mountains, and felt the pull again, stronger this time. She took a few steps along the glittering trail, which melted away behind her.

Diana didn't believe in magic, or magical sink holes, or alternate dimensions. There had to be logical explanations for wherever she was and however she'd gotten here. But the answers, she suspected, were on the other end of the trail.

She took out her phone and switched it on, only to see the NO SERVICE icon pop up. Wherever she was, she was too far from the cell towers —aka on her own. Following the trail without backup was stupid, of course. So was standing around doing nothing.

Diana holstered her Glock. She had ten rounds, and an extra clip in her jacket. She'd stopped carrying around a backup piece since department regulations had been changed to nix them, but she still had an EDC folding knife she kept tucked in her left boot. She'd gotten a brown belt in Judo before she'd had to drop out of training, and she took mandatory classes for the department every two years in defensive tactics.

Whatever waited for her on the other end of the trail, she would deal with it—and maybe find some answers, too.

With the sun setting, and no sign of any power poles, Diana had to move fast to cover the trail across the plain and up into the rocky slopes of the mountains. She ran for the first mile, slowed for a breather, and then jogged up onto the first rise of gray and white boulders. The cold air felt so good flooding her lungs that she broke into another run. The higher she went, the more the view improved. From what she could see she was on a peninsula, maybe even an island. It didn't look like Baja or Catalina, though. As the sky darkened to a rich orange-purple she glanced back to check for the lights from town, only to see nothing but more dusk.

No electricity. No palm trees. No cars.

Where the hell was she, Mexican cartel hell?

Once she reached the top of the first ridge Diana expected to be turned around. There was no way in hell she was rock-climbing without safety equipment. But then she saw a man-made passage cut through the stone into the mountain. She entered it, moving cautiously until she could see more of it, and then started jogging again.

How she was doing this with the knee she'd wrecked in college, especially after the year she'd had, Diana didn't know. Or care. She'd run for the rest of the night if it kept feeling this good.

She went another half-mile before the trail emptied onto a grassy plateau surrounding an enormous structure. Diana stared at it for a full minute before she leaned back against a wall of stone and rubbed her eyes. When she opened them again it was still there: a huge medieval castle, with towers and torches and a moat and big, burly-looking guards stationed at all the entrances. Guards wearing dark pants and light-colored plaids belted over their tunics, no less.

"Maybe I *am* hallucinating." She leaned out to

look at the castle again, which did not change into a big pink bunny and hop away. She bent over, let the blood rush to her head, and straightened. Still there. "Damn. Maybe I'm not."

Diana didn't have time to debate it to death. The last of the light was fading rapidly, and trying to navigate her way unnoticed into the big freaking castle would be next to impossible in the dark. Fortunately she had worn her navy suit and a dark blouse to work today, which would help conceal her as long as she stayed in the shadows.

She eyed the best approach and headed as silently as she could toward the side outer wall, waiting behind a big rock as the guards walking the top of the wall had gone to either end. She darted across the last expanse of grass and ducked into an arch, where she stepped back into the shadows as two men emerged from an open-ended passage.

"I'm no' saying you cannae look for your cousin, Seoc," the shorter, bald guy said in a heavy Scottish accent. "Only consider what the laird would be forced to do if you found him. Evander very nearly killed Raen to free a legion spy. He'll be put to death as a traitor."

His taller, hunched-shouldered companion

made a frustrated gesture. "I've naught else to do to redeem our name, Chieftain. He's forever disgraced the Talorc, but if I brought him back to face what he's done–"

"And Fiona Marphee?" the chieftain asked softly. "Would you wield the axe that ends Evander's lover?"

Diana watched them disappear into another passage before she emerged. Scottish guys in costumes at a monster castle talking about clans and spies and killing people with axes. Right.

If it was a movie set, where were the cameras and crew?

The tugging in her chest suddenly became a gripping, clawing compulsion that she couldn't resist. Diana swore silently as she gave into it and followed the trail, which took her through the passage and into a huge, empty room that looked like some sort of kitchen.

Whoever these guys were, they ate well. Baskets of fruits and vegetables had been stacked on shelves next to a fireplace so huge she could have parked her Caddy inside with room to spare. Inside it hung several huge, empty iron caldrons that looked like they could hold enough soup to feed an army. Wire baskets of eggs hung from hooks over huge sacks of oats and other grains. Wheels of cheese with hard rinds stood in high stacks, waiting to be cut open. She saw no fridge, stove or any other modern conveniences except for a giant-size stone sink. The smell of warm, sweet fruit made her peek inside one cabinet that had been filled with loaves of bread and some kind of jellied dessert in big clay pots.

The sound of voices growing louder made her duck behind the cabinet. A heartbeat later two more costumed actors entered the kitchen and walked across it toward the interior of the castle. Both of them were huge, well-developed men who looked as if they could kick anyone's ass without breaking a sweat. One was slightly smaller and moved like a dancer, which seemed odd for his bulky size. The other was a mountain of muscle on legs. From her position she couldn't see their faces, which oddly frustrated her.

"Wait," said a deep voice that rumbled. "Someone's been in here, my lord."

Diana flinched.

"Likely Neac, after another of Meg's pies now that she's abed," a mellow, amused voice answered. "Which is where I should be, as my lady awaits me in the tower. And you ken how she is when made to wait."

"Aye," the other man said. "Good-night, my lord."

Diana held her breath as the bigger man remained behind, and slowly approached the pie cabinet. Through the slats at the back she got a better look at how huge he was: easily a half-foot taller than her, and built like a Mack truck on steroids. His shaggy black hair had an odd silvery sheen to it, and one side of his face had been covered with primitive, jagged tattoos. Those had to be temporary, of course. No man so fine would tat up his face like that.

This one wasn't wearing a tartan, and his tunic clung to a vast, muscle-paved chest that, like his roof-beam shoulders, seemed to go on forever. Whatever workout he favored had done wonders for his physique. His biceps looked bigger than her head, and his thighs were like ripped tree trunks. His scent rolled around the cabinet and doused her with a smell exactly like the air after a midnight rain storm: cool and dark and clean.

He was standing too far away for her to smell him, she realized.

Why do I suddenly have a nose like a bloodhound?

The dragging sensation inside her suddenly jerked hard, and then dissolved into a wave of elation. It felt a little like the surge of emotion she experienced whenever she found one of her victims alive and safe, only more intense. Which, since he wasn't lost, and she didn't know him from Adam, was completely ridiculous.

Stop being distracted by the big man, Diana chided herself. *You're here to find Kinley.*

The man frowned, and took a step back, glancing over his shoulder. "Neac? Come out, man. I'll no' tell Meg you were filching."

He reached out toward her with one giant paw, and closed the door she'd left open. After that he waited for a long moment, breathing in deeply, before he shook his head, swung back around and retreated into the castle.

All the breath whooshed out of Diana's lungs as she sagged against the rough brick wall.

The weird pulling sensation also evaporated from inside her, allowing her to gather her scattered brains. Whoever and whatever the big guy was, he wasn't her problem.

She remained in her hiding spot until she felt reasonably sure no one else would walk in, and then performed a quick recon of the area. She might be spotted if she went after the men, and since she had no backup it seemed safer to stay out of sight. She found the entrance to another passage that appeared deserted, and followed it to a set of stone steps, which she climbed up to the next floor. There she followed another passage that allowed her to look down on a cavernous area where several dozen men were standing, sitting and talking.

Most wore variations of the guard's costumes, but the big man who had almost found her was greeting two much smaller men dressed in long, plain woolen robes, who had been escorted in by a pair of the guards. The most striking thing about the room was that there were no women in it at all.

Beyond them, the golden trail glittered, seemingly unnoticed, and led through an arch into a tower with a staircase.

My lady awaits me in the tower, the man with the mellow voice had said.

Diana sized up her options, and returned the way she came to look for a way to get to the tower.

Chapter Three

ANOTHER DAY RETREATED over the horizon, drawing the dusky hem of twilight's coverlet over its sunny head. In the great hall Tharaen Aber watched the night guards on their way to relieve the day watch as they paused to light torches in the flames of the massive hearth. The strangeness he had felt in the kitchen still itched at the back of his neck, as if prodding him to return and perform a search. Yet he knew he would find nothing but foods and pies and dishes. No outsider could have entered the stronghold without first being seen by the curtain wall patrols or the entry guards.

"Fair evening, Seneschal Aber," one of the guards said as he passed Raen, and bobbed his head.

Raen returned the nod, feeling again the uneasy weight of the position thrust upon him. "And to you, Fergus Uthar."

While serving as bodyguard to Lachlan McDonnel, laird of the McDonnel clan, Raen had never given much thought to the work involved with looking after Dun Aran, the clan's stronghold. Hidden for a thousand and two hundred years in the Black Cuillin mountain range on the Isle of Skye, the castle served as home and outpost for the clan of immortal highlanders. Built by the McDonnels in a giant crater hidden within the keel of stony ridges, the castle required constant attendance by hundreds of mortal retainers and servants. Raen himself devoted nearly every waking moment to overseeing the work of the household since the former seneschal, Evander Talorc, had betrayed the clan.

"Seneschal."

Raen turned to see a patrol team escorting a pair of robed men between them, and went to meet them. Both of the druids looked tired and untidy. "Fair evening, Master Flen, Ovate Lusk. What brings you so late to the castle?"

The older, gray-haired druid drew himself up

like an offended rooster. "We've urgent matters to discuss with Lachlan McDonnel. Where is he?"

Everything Bhaltair Flen wanted done, Raen suspected, was urgent. "The laird has retired for the evening, Master Flen. If you wish to remain and speak to him on the morrow, I can offer you lodging."

"This cannae wait on the laird's leisure." The old druid's flowing sleeve snapped as he made an impatient gesture. "Step aside."

"Master Flen." Neacal Uthar strode over with a brimming tankard. "You're looking parched. Here, have some ale."

As the chieftain distracted the old druid, his younger companion spoke quickly to Raen.

"We've reports of groups of undead moving on the mainland," Cailean Lusk said. His boyish face and soft, innocent eyes did not reflect the ancient soul behind them. "'Tis the first sightings of them since they vanished last year, Master Aber. The conclave feels 'tis a matter of great urgency to learn where they go, and what their intentions may be."

"So does the clan," Raen said. "If you'll convince your master to sit, I'll go and speak to the laird."

He turned and headed for the tower stairs, but as he ducked under the arch he saw a pair of long, shapely legs in dark blue trews disappearing up the steps. The scent of spiced honey wafted over him as it had in the kitchens, and he hurried after the figure.

The tall, lean stranger wore a strange cap, and in one hand held an oddly-shaped hunk of metal. When Raen's boot slid on one of the steps the stranger turned and pointed the object at him. He frowned as he took in the sleek body under the clothing before he looked into large eyes the same light violet shade of thyme flowers. The high cheekbones and regal nose might have belonged to a man, but the lovely lips, fashioned for endless kissing, said woman. When she lifted her arm he saw her strange, boxy coat tighten over the curves of her breasts, confirming her sex.

Whoever she was, she had the face of a goddess.

"Stop right there," the woman said in a commanding voice that seemed to hum inside his bones. "San Diego PD. Hands where I can see them. *Now.*"

Raen obliged and showed her his hands. The woman's accent sounded like Kinley's, and her bizarre clothing was like nothing he'd ever seen. What chilled his blood were the words she'd said: San Diego. Kinley had come from the same place.

"My name is Tharaen Aber," he said, keeping his voice low and gentle. "You've naught to fear, my lady."

Her dark red brows rose. "Cute. I'm a cop, Mr. Aber, not a lady. What is this place?"

That he didn't know what *cop* meant told him that she had likely come from the future, but her violet eyes seemed to reach into him as if she could see his insides. Recalling how the laird's wife had behaved when she had crossed over into their time, he took care to choose his words.

"It is called Dun Aran. You are among friends here, my, ah, Mistress."

"I don't have any friends into Dungeons and Dragons, and I'm not your mistress." She came down toward him a few steps. "Where is Captain Kinley Chandler?"

Before Raen could reply footsteps thudded behind him, and he saw Bhaltair approaching. "Master Flen, please wait in the great hall."

"You'll no' delay me again." The old druid's eyes widened as soon as he saw the woman from the future, and his expression filled with shock. "No. It cannae be."

"Afraid it can, old guy. Lieutenant Diana Burke, San Diego Missing Persons Unit." She took out a folded piece of leather, unfolded it, and held it up to show a gleaming oval of stamped metal and a printed card. "You can go right back out the way you came." She lifted her chin in the direction of the hall, and then fixed her lovely eyes on Raen. "*You* are taking me upstairs. Now move it, nice and slow."

Raen nodded, and started to climb up to her. Instead of returning to the hall, however, the old druid followed him.

"Hey, old guy," Diana said to Bhaltair as Raen joined her. She made a prodding motion with the metal object. "This is police business. Go wait with the rest of the extras."

The old druid seemed to snap out of his trance, and his face reddened. "How dare you speak to me like that? I am Bhaltair Flen—"

"And I really don't care," she said flatly. "Get your ass downstairs, pronto."

At that moment Raen snatched the object from her hand, only to find himself slammed back against the tower wall. Diana kicked, punched, and rammed an elbow into him before he could take a breath, and tried to take back the metal hunk. It bucked in Raen's hand as a terrible explosion shattered the air, and filled it with a burnt stink. He looked down to see the old druid falling to his knees and clutching his arm as blood from a tiny hole in his robe soaked his sleeve.

Chapter Four

꧁❀꧂

C AILEAN CAME RUSHING up the
stairs to catch the conclavist, and gave
Raen a look of horror.

"Take him into the hall, Ovate," Raen said.

He snatched the weapon from Diana, which
felt hot on one end, and wrapped his arm around
her waist. Tossing her over his shoulder, he
hurried up the stairs.

Lachlan, wearing only a pair of hastily-
donned trews, met him in the corridor outside his
bed chamber.

"What made that banger?" the laird
demanded. His gaze shifted to Diana's writhing,
kicking body, and his eyes widened. "Oh, fack
me, no."

"'Twas this that made the noise." With some

difficulty Raen passed the weapon to the laird. "Have a care, my lord. It put a hole through Master Flen." He grimaced as a boot slammed into his hip. "She calls herself Lieutenant Diana Burke from San Diego. She mentioned a unit of missing persons. Another soldier, I think."

"I'm a cop, you idiot, and if you don't put me down, right this minute," Diana said, her voice sounding almost reasonable and calm, "I'll shoot a hole through your balls."

"I'll keep the hole-maker," Lachlan said and nodded toward the room at the end of the corridor. "Put her in there, and see if you can calm her. I'll send Tormod to stand guard."

Raen kept tight hold on Diana as he carried her down to the room once occupied by the laird's wife, ducked inside and shoved the door shut with his boot. As soon as he placed her on her feet she attacked him with another flurry of punches and kicks, but this time he expected them, and easily parried each blow.

Diana moved away from him as if they were dancing, holding her fists up and ready to strike as she made a quick scan of the room.

"You're going down for assaulting a police officer," she said. "Do you really want to add aggravated kidnapping charges, and whatever else I can nail you for? Because a year or two in county jail is nothing compared to twenty-five to life at the state pen."

"Lieutenant," Raen said, guessing that using her rank rather than her name showed more respect, "if you will stop attacking me, we can talk."

"Your lord guy is sending someone to stand guard," she said nodding toward the corridor. "That's false imprisonment. Think about what you're doing here, Tharaen. Twenty-five to life in a tiny little cell, eating crap food and fighting very bad guys in the yard. Big as you are? Every damn day."

"That may happen in San Diego." Since there was no lock on the door, Raen shifted back and leaned against it. "But you are no' there anymore, Lieutenant."

"Really." Diana's gaze kept shifting to every object around her. "Where do you think we are?"

"Dinnae do it, lass," Raen warned her as he saw her stance shift.

But as soon as the last word left his lips she lunged at him. Knowing she might shatter a bone this time, he met her halfway and spun with her in his arms, using the momentum to fling both of them onto the bed. Their combined weight made the lower frame collapse beneath them, and he rolled atop her, pinning her under him to prevent another attempt at escape.

"Be still now," he said. He removed the odd hat that had slipped down over her face, and a long, thick mass of streaked light red hair fell around her face. He'd never seen lovelier locks on any woman, and couldn't resist the urge to touch it. "Why do you hide all this glory? 'Tis like copper and gold made silk."

"I don't," Diana said and turned her face into her hair, closed her eyes for a long moment, and then regarded him. "I didn't have long hair before I came here. I haven't for years. None of this is real," she murmured, sounding confused, and then drew in her lower lip to worry it with her teeth. "Can't be. It's impossible."

When she started struggling again Raen shifted. "Dinnae try to toss me. You cannae."

"Yeah, I'm getting that." She gripped his shoulders, giving him a tentative push. "I can't even budge you. Why do you feel like you're made of concrete?"

"'Tis how I am in battle," Raen said and paused.

He had forgotten what it was to have a woman under him. Diana was nearly as tall as he, and her limbs felt sleek with tight muscle, but with every breath she took her breasts pressed against his chest. His blood went hot and thick as he drew one of her hands from his shoulder, and pressed it back against the coverlet.

"You shouldnae fight me, lass."

"Then help me," she said quickly. "Wake me up or talk me out of this or–" She flinched as he tore down the bed drapes. "Oh, no. Don't you even *think* it."

Raen controlled her writhing form with his body weight as he ripped the drapes into strips and tied her wrists to the bed posts. Only when she was firmly bound did he rise and move to the bottom of the bed to catch her kicking legs and bind her ankles together.

"If this is real—and the jury's still out on that —you're going to regret this," she promised him.

"Aye." Looking down at her, he already did.

The chamber door opened, and Tormod Liefson entered with a wary look.

"The laird said I should guard the wench."

He glanced past Raen and grimaced. "Fack us all. Another one?"

"Say naught to her," Raen warned in a low voice as he passed the Norseman. "Stand guard outside. I'll return with the laird once we've seen to Master Flen."

"Take whiskey," Tormod suggested. "And some good, strong rope."

❧

WHEN RAEN WENT down to the great hall he found it filled with clansmen, most of whom had armed themselves, and the laird and lady, who sat listening to Cailean relate what had happened on the stairs. He spotted the older druid seated in a chair covered with cushions, where Neac and some of his tribe were attempting to treat his wound.

"Look," Bhaltair said, gripping his elbow as he held out his arm to show Raen as he approached them. "There is a hole in my flesh. It goes straight through, from front to back. I believe that vicious, ill-mannered harpy meant to spit me like some great roast. Look at how she maimed me with her black magic."

"Now, there, Master Flen," Neac said as he urged him to lower his arm. "'Tis but a flesh wound. We'll see to bathing and binding it for you."

"Are you mad? I may be crippled. If the wound festers, I could lose my arm," the druid said, grabbing the wound and then releasing a groan of pain before he called out. "Cailean, attend me now."

Raen gave the ovate a sympathetic look as they exchanged places.

"My lord," Raen said to Lachlan, "the druids came with news of sightings of the legion. Master Flen was coming to speak with you when he found me with the lady on the stairs. I believe she is another soldier from San Diego." He related everything Diana had said to him, and then asked, "Is she someone you ken from your time?"

"No, we've never met," Kinley said, but glanced back at the tower, worry plain in her light blue eyes. "She's not a soldier, either. A police officer is someone who enforces the laws. Like the king's sheriffs do now on the mainland. A missing persons unit looks for people who have disappeared without an explanation. The lieutenant must be investigating my case."

Lachlan produced the weapon. "And this?"

"This is a gun." His wife gingerly took it from him and thumbed something on the back of it. "It's a weapon from my time. I've put the safety on, so it won't fire again until I take it off. Ah, it fires bullets, pieces of metal, that shoot through the air too fast for you to see. When the bullets strike a body, they bore through it." She thought for a moment. "It's sort of like a tiny cannon."

"Gods," Lachlan muttered. His expression turned grim as he regarded the weapon. "But why would this police officer shoot Bhaltair?"

"'Twas an accident, my lord," Raen said quickly. "I took the gun from Diana, and while she tried to retrieve it from me, it fired a bullet at him."

"And that's why we're keeping the gun's safety on," Kinley said, and looked at her husband. "Lieutenant Burke must have crossed over through the oak grove where I did. I just don't know why she'd still be looking for me. It's been a year since I left home."

"She did ask after you by name, my lady," Raen told her.

"Kinley and I will speak to the Lieutenant," Lachlan told him, and nodded at Bhaltair. "After we explain the accident to Master Flen, and hear this news about the legion."

Raen accompanied the laird and his lady over to the druids, and found Cailean using whiskey to clean the wound. Bhaltair lay on his side, his pale, sweaty face drawn with pain, but as soon as he saw Lachlan he bolted upright.

"You must deliver this female to me immediately, my lord," the druid demanded. "The ovate and I will take her to be judged by the conclave at once."

"Master Flen, please permit me to explain," Raen said, and quickly related what had happened in his struggle to take the weapon from Diana. "Lieutenant Burke didnae deliberately shoot you, sir. If anyone is to blame for your wound, 'tis me."

"Nonsense. 'Twas her weapon, in her hand. I saw it with my own eyes." Bhaltair's color returned to flood his face. "You heard how she spoke to me. I wouldnae address a dog with so little consideration or respect."

Raen suspected the old druid's pride had been injured along with his arm. As a member of the conclave, Bhaltair held the second-highest rank among his people, and had always been treated by the laird and the McDonnel clan with the utmost respect. At times he could become very unpleasant over anything he perceived as a slight. Yet something else seemed to be goading him as well. He behaved as if he had been offended, but the outrage in his eyes looked almost like hatred.

"I regret that you came to harm here, Master Flen," Lachlan said. "But this female crossed over from the future, as Kinley did. Mayhap by accident, while she was in the grove, seeking to find my wife. While she may be druid kind, we cannae punish the lass for being ignorant of your position, or for attending to her duty."

Now Raen recalled that only druid kind could use the oak groves to travel through time, which meant that Diana Burke shared her bloodline with the magic folk. That also made her answerable to the druid conclave.

"Very well," the druid said stiffly. "If she came by accident, then she doesnae belong here, and must be sent back. Cailean and I will see to it. Fetch her to me now."

"Bhaltair, you are in no condition to drag a frightened, unwilling woman all over Scotland," Kinley told him. "Now what's this news about the legion?" She looked at Cailean.

"Our allies to the south report that the undead have been seen traveling from the lowlands," the ovate said. "They move in groups of eight to the north. The conclave thought you might know what that meant, my lord."

"Eight is a contubernium," Lachlan murmured, and then said to his wife, "'Tis the smallest legion formation. Mayhap they are being commanded to gather for some purpose in the north."

"'Twas also how the Ninth moved the entire legion across Caledonia to attack us here," Raen reminded the laird. "I remember the tribune taunting you about expecting to fight a thousand men, when he had gathered six thousand to slay us."

Kinley took hold of Lachlan's hand. "Since that attack ended up making the clan immortal, and the legion our undead enemies for all eternity, we might want to jump on this."

"Aye, you must learn their purpose, my lord," Bhaltair said. "Which you cannae do if you are trifling with this outsider woman. Bring her to Cailean, and he will take charge of her."

"Since I'm the reason Lieutenant Burke came here, I'd like to speak with her before she returns to San Diego," Kinley said. "Otherwise she could come back again, and bring reinforcements."

"Agreed," Lachlan said. "Raen, arrange an escort to take Master Flen and Ovate Lusk back to their settlement. For now, we will keep Diana Burke here at the stronghold."

"I think I should also stay," Cailean said quickly before he turned to the old druid. "With your permission, Master, so that I may be available, should circumstances require my assistance."

The old druid exchanged a strange look with his acolyte, and then seemed to settle into a calmer mood. "Yes, I think that wise. The laird's men will look after me. Should you need my counsel, you may send a message by dove."

The prospect of Diana staying at Dun Aran made Raen feel a strange mixture of relief and dread. He tried to shake it off, and caught Kinley giving him an odd look. "Is there something else, my lady?"

She smiled a little. "It's just your face. I thought I saw your ink glitter for a second."

Chapter Five

✦❦✦

THE MOON ROSE, full and frosty over the vast acres of woodlands surrounding the enormous country estate. Tribune Quintus Seneca looked up at the cold eye of night as he walked past the castle's new guards, whose bloodless flesh made them appear like statues instead of men. As they saluted him he saw the hunger burning in their black eyes, but it did not trouble him. Over the last year his undead army had endured meager rations and everything else Quintus had asked of them.

Soon enough they would be rewarded.

A centurion intercepted him at the threshold, and brought his arm up diagonally across his chest.

"Tribune, the last cohorts have arrived."

"Assemble the men. I will address them shortly."

Once the centurion had departed Quintus continued through the hall and entered the buttery. From there he walked down into the labyrinth of wine racks, brine barrels and cheese presses that crowded the lower levels. Once past the household stores he descended again into the torch-lit second level, formerly the dungeon, which he had ordered his men to prepare as his command center and personal quarters.

As he changed out of his tunic and trousers into his formal uniform, he heard rustling sounds coming from the room that served as his bed chamber. He wondered if the countess would be as well this night as she had been the last.

I was a fool to trifle with her, Quintus thought as he finished dressing by donning his armor, and clipping his paludamentum to his right shoulder with a simple fibula. Before they had been cursed, a tribune wearing the red cloak in front of his troops was a signal that the legion was being sent into battle. Now he wore it every time he spoke to the men.

They had fought long and hard to survive. Victory now awaited, just over the horizon.

"Who is out there?" a plaintive voice called.

Quintus entered the bed chamber, and looked down at the beautiful mortal woman tied naked to the bed. The laird's wife was the loveliest mortal female he had ever seen, and after they had taken the castle last night he could not resist using her as his blood thrall. She had begged him to stop, and offered him instead the use of her divine body. Although he never toyed with mortal women, her beauty made it impossible for him to resist. Later, while she lay sleeping in his arms, Quintus had stared at the bite marks on her long, white throat. He hated seeing her perfection spoiled, and had used a little of his own blood to heal them.

"There you are, my master," the countess said, her languid voice filled with longing. "I have waited all day for you to return. Willnae you have me again?"

He frowned. Blood thralls rarely resisted after they had been used, but that was from weakness and shock. "Why would you wish me to?"

"I want you," she said and rolled her shoulders to jut her breasts in an inviting manner. "Please, touch me."

He felt his cock swell as he sat down beside the countess, and fondled her breasts until she moaned. Fucking her last night had given him almost as much pleasure as the sweet, hot blood that pulsed through her veins.

"Are you not afraid of me?"

She smiled as if she were in love with his every word.

"I wish only to serve you, Master. I will spread my legs for you, so that you might fuck me and drink from me again." Her dark eyes shifted toward the cords binding her to the bed posts. "Release me and I will."

Quintus leaned closer and saw that her green eyes had darkened considerably since last night. If he had drained her to the point of death and then forced her to drink his own blood, that would have changed her into an undead. But all he had done was use her. He rose from the bed and used his dagger to cut through her bonds.

"On your knees before me," he ordered.

The countess flung herself from the bed to the floor, where she knelt and looked up at him with visible adoration.

"Do you wish to put your cock in my mouth? I will suck it and drink from you, my master."

"Guard," he shouted, and when his men hurried in he gestured to one of them. "Stand over her," he ordered, "and take out your shaft." When the guard did as ordered, Quintus said to the countess, "I want you to suck him."

She pursed her lips, then turned her head and began to fellate the guard.

Quintus watched her suck the man until he came, and ordered her to do the same to the second guard. He then commanded her to let them use her mouth and quim at the same time while he watched. She obeyed with such obvious pleasure that it could not be an act, but he was still not yet convinced.

"Bring the lowest, most odorous servant in the castle to me," Quintus instructed the guards, who left and returned a few minutes later with a filthy, terrified swineherd. "Strip him."

Once the shivering man was naked, he saw the open pox sores around his groin, and knew that would have to be too much for the countess to continue her farce.

"Give yourself to this man," he told her.

Without hesitation the beautiful woman hurried to the bed, spreading herself there as if for a refined, perfumed lover. The bulge-eyed swineherd had to be dragged by the guards to her. But once they shoved him on top of the countess he began to use her vigorously. All the while she kissed and caressed his dirty, scabrous body with loving hands.

As the swineherd slobbered kisses over the countess's white throat, Quintus remembered the minor healing he had performed. Could his blood have caused her to behave like this?

As the guards watched the mortals, the tribune went back upstairs and ordered the countess's husband brought to him. The earl, who had been beaten bloody by the legion as they stormed the castle, had to be dragged into the great hall.

He swore loudly as soon as he saw Quintus. "You facking monstrous demon, where is my wife?"

"You would not believe me if I told you." To the guard Quintus said, "Bring him here to me."

The earl struggled as Quintus sank his fangs into his wrist and drank from his veins.

"You'd better kill me now, you bastart," the earl yelled, "for I'll cut out your black heart the moment I've a chance."

The mortal continued to threaten and rage as Quintus dragged his own thumb over the tip of his fang. He smeared the bite marks he had left on the earl's wrist with his own blood, and watched them slowly heal and disappear. Silence filled the great hall as the furious mortal went still and quiet. He stared at Quintus as if he were startled. The earl's expression slowly softened, and his mouth curved.

"I shouldnae have fought you, my laird," the earl said. "Forgive me." He bowed his head.

"What do you wish to do now?" Quintus asked the earl.

"Naught but what will please you, my laird." The earl's blue eyes began to darken, and his ruddy skin took on a distinct pallor. "Command me and 'twill be done."

"Why don't you go and share your wife with her new lover?" Quintus snapped, and said to the guards, "Take him down to my chambers and put him with the other two until I return."

As he strode out to the front lawn, where the legion's cohorts stood waiting, Quintus tried to imagine what would happen when the proud earl found a swineherd fucking his wife. He almost felt sorry for her.

Quintus took his position before the legion.

Brutus Ficini, his most trusted centurion, shouted, *"Noto. Animus attentus."*

Thousands of gauntlets slammed against

chests as the men of the Ninth Legion came to attention, their pale flesh and black eyes absolutely still. Since Gaius Lucinius's death they had been forced to follow Quintus' strict orders, even when it defied their undead nature. But now he had the pleasure of rewarding them all for it.

"Brothers," Quintus said, his voice piercing the stillness. "I am honored by your loyalty, and humbled by your diligence. The sacrifices you have made have preserved this legion entirely. As my ancestor, Marcus Annaeus Seneca once wrote, every new beginning comes from some other beginning's end. This night I have learned that our scouts have prevailed at last. They have found a well-concealed, easily defensible location in the north territory that can serve as the Ninth's new castrum. There, with your help, we will rebuild our stronghold. *Centurio, fere spectare.*"

The long line of sixty centurions within the legion took one step forward, turned and faced their cohorts.

"Your centurions have your orders," Quintus told the men. "Travel quickly and quietly. We will next meet at the northern encampment. *Aquilifer.*"

The standard bearer stepped forward, and

lifted his pole to raise the legion's golden eagle high in the air.

"Rome that ruled the world is no more," Quintus said. He despised reminding the men of that bitter fact, but for once it could serve another purpose. "We, too, have been cast into darkness, but we have never surrendered. I am no god, or emperor, but like all of you a soldier who has fought long and hard for what is rightfully ours. We will take back dominion over this land." He lifted an arm, saluting them. *"Ave Legio nota Hispania!"*

The men returned the salute, but they shouted, *"Ave Seneca! Ave Seneca!"*

Once the men were dispatched by their centurions to make the long journey by different routes, Quintus instructed his own guard to ready their horses. His last task was to return to the cellar, where the earl, his countess and the swineherd awaited him.

Both guards looked confused, but snapped to attention as soon as he entered the bed chamber. Quintus saw why as he took in the strange tableau on the bed.

The earl had his wife under him as he busily worked himself in and out of her body. At the same time the swineherd stood beside the bed, the countess's hair in his fists as he made use of her mouth. The countess lay unresisting, her slumberous eyes brightening with pleasure as she saw Quintus.

"Keep sucking him, my lady," the earl said as he reared up. He jerked out his cock as he watched Quintus, and then shook as he came all over his wife's breasts and belly. As the swineherd stiffened and grunted, the nobleman climbed off the bed and tugged up his trews. "She's well-primed for you now, my lord."

"Take the servant out of here, and send Ficini to me," Quintus told the guards before he asked the earl, "You allowed your wife to service a filthy, pox-ridden peasant while you took her. Why?"

The earl looked confused. "You told me to, my lord."

"If I say to strangle the life out of her, you would?" Quintus demanded. "You would kill the woman you love for me?"

"Of course," the other man said, smiling in the same adoring way that his wife had. "I would do anything for you, my lord."

"I do not believe you." Quintus strode out into the next room, kicking the door shut behind him and pacing until Ficini arrived. "Something has happened."

Once he told the centurion about the nobles' bizarre behavior, Ficini said, "Some of the men have had similar incidents with mortals they have used and healed. They follow them, and behave as if they are devoted slaves. They have helped to hide the men during the day, lure other mortals for them to feed on, and even kill their own kind to prevent them from raising the alarm."

Last year, after the disastrous destruction of the legion's underground lair, Quintus had been forced to disperse his men to search for a new stronghold. To prevent the McDonnel clan from tracking their movements, he'd also issued orders for the legion to stop killing mortals altogether, take only enough blood from them to survive another day, and conceal any sign that they had been used for blood. Smearing a bite wound with a little undead blood made the mortal's injury vanish.

Just as he had used his blood to heal the countess's throat.

"Do you mean to tell me that we can make willing slaves out of mortals?" Quintus demanded. "That we have wasted twelve centuries draining them to death, when we might have enthralled armies of them to do our bidding?"

"I can repeat only what has been reported to me," Ficini said. He looked uncomfortable now. "I did always wonder how Tribune Gaius Lucinius had such control over his blood thralls."

"Before that druid woman burned him to death, Gaius believed himself a god," Quintus said. "He ordered us to use mortals until they were dead. I despised him, but if he knew about this healing enthrallment… No, I cannot believe it. Even Gaius would not have been that foolish."

"Perhaps these mortals went insane," the centurion said carefully, "and the men mistook it for enthrallment."

"Then I will demonstrate it for you, and you may tell me what it is." He gestured for the centurion to follow him into the bed chamber, and came to an abrupt halt.

"I have strangled her for you, my lord," the earl said as he dropped his wife's limp body to the floor. He pointed proudly at the mottled bruises marring her throat. "Now do you believe me?"

Chapter Six

✿❀✿

WITH HER TEETH Diana finished tugging the knot around her right wrist loose, and cupped her hand. Twisting it slowly one way and then the other, she worked her hand free of the makeshift restraint. Keeping close watch on the door, she untied the other wrist and then freed her ankles. A quick, silent search of the room turned up several things she could use as weapons. She settled on a long, sturdy rod with a crude hook carved on one end. She'd batted .411 when she'd played softball in college, so kneecapping the next person through the door would be no problem.

Unless it was Raen Aber, and his gorgeous, unyielding body. What kind of man turned into a walking brick wall during a fight?

Once Diana armed herself she looked for another way out. The narrow open slit that served as the only window seemed promising, if she could squeeze through it. She got her head and arm out, at which point she saw the two-hundred-foot drop down into the ominously black pit surrounding the base of the castle. While she'd survived that last, horrific fall from Horsethief Canyon, she had no way of knowing if her monumental luck would repeat itself.

Her hair fell in her eyes as she came out of the window, and when she pushed it back she couldn't help threading her fingers through it. Her hair hadn't felt this thick and silky since she'd been in the academy. Back then she'd chopped it all off when her firearms instructor had threatened to shave her head if she didn't keep it out of her face on the range. After that keeping it short had been convenient. More recently, it hadn't been a matter of choice.

God, she'd missed having long hair. She wanted to brush it and curl it and she would—as soon as she woke up from this dreamy nightmare.

Low voices spoke outside the door to the room, and galvanized Diana into action. She positioned herself beside the hinges, adjusting her grip on the rod until it felt balanced. As it opened she shifted, ready to swing. The woman who walked in was slender, golden-haired and practically glowing with health. She also looked exactly like Kinley Chandler before an explosion knocked her face-first into a rescue helicopter.

Diana froze as she looked into the white-streaked blue eyes she'd only seen in case file photos.

"Captain Chandler?"

"Yes," Kinley said as her gaze shifted to the rod. "Lachlan, you should stay in the hall."

"And what fun would that be, my wife?" A man almost as big as Raen stepped inside, and immediately shoved Kinley behind him. "Put it down now, lass."

"Be happy to," Diana said and could see the dangerous gleam in Lachlan's dark eyes, but he didn't worry her. Seeing Kinley Chandler healed of her very serious, life-threatening injuries as if they'd never happened, on the other hand, scared the snot out of her. "Soon as Captain Chandler explains why she looks like that, where I am, who these guys are, and how the hell I got here. Oh, and if you can define what, exactly, made my hair grow out two feet in a couple hours, that would be great, too."

"If you'll hand over that rod to my husband," Kinley countered, "I'll tell you everything."

Diana didn't want to let go, but she suspected if she didn't the big guy would take it from her. "On one condition: no one ties me to the bed again unless I ask them to."

Lachlan exchanged a long, silent look with his wife before he said, "Agreed."

"Okay," Diana said and handed him the rod, and felt her knees shake as the rush of adrenalin wore off. "Before anything else, how's the old guy?"

"He's no' happy, but the wound isnae serious." The laird hesitated before he added, "Raen claimed 'twas an accident."

"The gun went off as we were wrestling for it. If I'd meant to shoot him, he'd be dead." She leaned up against the wall and regarded Kinley. "Any time now, Captain."

Kinley briefed her on the situation, if anyone could call being transported back in time to a fourteenth century castle on a Scottish island that.

According to her the big guys weren't actors, but a clan of actual highlanders. Their mission was to fight Roman soldiers that had been turned by a curse into vampires that were called the undead.

Struggling to keep a straight face got easier for Diana as the captain described how she'd fallen in love with the laird of the McDonnel clan. Diana had no problem believing that. Lachlan was almost as hot as Raen. But she still felt as if she'd landed in the middle of a medieval fantasy novel. If an actual dragon had popped into the room, she probably would have taken it in stride.

She also had the feeling that Kinley wasn't telling her everything. Every time she mentioned the McDonnels her body language shifted subtly, as if she were concealing something about the clan.

Probably the dragons, Diana thought. "Look, that's a really cool story, but I have photos of you from last year when you came back from Afghanistan. I know how badly you were hurt. If we're in the fourteenth century, then why aren't you scar-faced and thumping around on a wooden leg?"

"Crossing over into this time healed me

completely," Kinley finally said. "The portal in the oak grove did it somehow—like making your hair grow so fast. But the changes don't stick if I return to the future. I know because I did once, briefly, and all my injuries came back."

"That sucks," Diana muttered suddenly thinking of Baby sitting in the visitor's parking lot at the entrance to the canyon. She rubbed the back of her neck. In a strange way her Caddy had always been the embodiment of hope to her. Now she felt a feeble spark of that hope again, minus the car. "You had to make a tough choice."

Kinley's smile turned rueful as she touched her cheek. "I like having my face back again, but that's not the reason I've stayed." She gave her husband a smile.

"I get that," Diana said. She had been keeping one eye on the laird, who should have been watching her, but was too busy looking at his wife. "What I don't understand is why your tree portal brought me here. Is it because I was looking for you, or I just stepped in the wrong spot?"

"We dinnae ken how the portals work," Lachlan said. "But the druids have told us only their kind can use them to pass through time. You must have their blood, as Kinley does."

"My family came from Skye," his wife added. "Do you have anyone in your family with Scottish lineage?"

"I don't know. I grew up in foster care," Diana admitted. She regarded the laird. "Listen, I know I just dropped in on you guys, literally, but now that I'm here, I'd like to stay for a bit. Just to be sure Kinley is all right, and that I'm not drugged or anything. That be okay with you?"

Lachlan studied her face for a long moment. "I've no doubt 'twould gladden my wife, but you'll be missed by your people."

"I'm not married or involved, and I don't have kids. I work too many hours to make friends." The laird was definitely not an idiot, but over the last year Diana had learned to lie like a campaigning politician. "I won't tell anyone about this place, or what happened to Kinley after she came here."

He smiled a little, but his dark eyes remained wary.

"I'll have some conditions of my own, Lieutenant. You cannae use your gun weapon, ever, or roam about Dun Aran alone."

She could stay, Diana thought, and felt her heart skip like a little kid in her chest.

"Sounds fair, as long as I'm not locked up in here all day."

"As long as Raen or Tormod remains with you, then aye," the laird said. "You are our guest."

Chapter Seven

RAEN WATCHED THE laird and his wife walk down to the edge of Loch Sìorraidh before he returned to the stronghold and asked the clan's chatelaine, Margret Talley, to make up a tray for Diana. He had been charged with looking after her as well as Dun Aran until Lachlan and Kinley returned from their meeting with the druid conclave.

"I wonder if ye might share blood with this one, Seneschal," the old woman said as she filled two mugs with her morning honey brew and handed one to him. "I've no' yet set eyes on her, but the men say she's a giantess."

"She's taller than most lasses, but she's no' an Aber." He plucked an apple from one of the fruit baskets and added it to the tray. "All our women were dark."

"Still, she'd suit ye," Meg said and piled some oatcakes in a basket and handed it to him. "If ye were tempted by all that pretty copper-gold hair." When he didn't reply she gave him a sideways glance. "'Tis fifty years now. Ye've mourned long enough, lad."

"Aye," he sighed. The reminder of his poor, lost wife Bradana should have hurt, but for once Raen felt only a distant sadness. "Only the lady will no' be staying." He finished his brew and picked up the tray. "Dinnae worry on me, Meg."

"I've no' the time for it." She flapped her apron at him. "Go on with ye."

As he crossed the great hall to climb the tower stairs, Raen felt tempted to summon Tormod Liefson again. He'd managed to avoid Diana by keeping busy with the household, and Lachlan had assigned Tormod to serve as the lieutenant's guard and escort, which had not made the Norseman at all happy.

"She's a stag in a wench skin, I swear it," Tormod had told him flatly last night, after Diana had retired. "She demands to run every dawn five miles, whatever they are. I must dash after her through the glen and up the south pass, where the rocks are slippery. I'll break my head open one morning, I ken it."

Raen had never known a female to run unless chased.

"Does she mean to escape?"

"No, for she always turns about and runs back again," Tormod said and took a long swallow from his tankard of ale. "And she's ever telling me to spot her with the grain sacks."

Now Raen felt completely mystified. "Spot? Do you mean watch?"

"Aye, while I stand over her ready to grab the sacks, should she falter. She carries them up from the kitchens, and you ken how Meg loves filching," Tormod said darkly. "Only she doesnae eat the grain, or cook it. She lifts it up and down until her arms shake."

Raen nodded, although he had no idea what the Norseman meant.

"And how do you help her?"

"The wench never needs my help. She's arms like a good archer, with the muscles showing, and yet still works them." The Norseman released a belch and sighed. "'Tis fashing me daft."

Raen knew he could no longer put off shep-

herding Diana, so he released Tormod from his
guard duty that night. It would be as it had been
with Kinley those first days, the big man decided
as he approached her chamber. He had only to
keep her from harm.

"Come in," Diana called out after Raen
knocked.

As soon as Raen stepped inside he nearly
dropped the tray. Diana was almost naked and
upside-down. She had somehow balanced on both
hands, which she had pressed on the floor, and
curled her body over backward so that her toes
hovered just in front of her nose.

"Lieutenant."

"Relax, Big Man." She slowly bent in the
opposite direction until her feet touched the floor,
at which point she rose up to a standing position.
"It's called yoga. Specifically, the *taraksvasana*, the
handstand scorpion."

Raen couldn't take his eyes from her. The only
things she wore on her long, beautiful body were
tiny trews made of black lace and an equally
scanty, skin-tight lace band that barely covered
her breasts.

"See anything you like?" she asked, sounding
amused now.

He set down the tray and pulled off his tartan, averting his gaze as he draped the plaid over her shoulders.

"You should have told me to wait so you could dress."

"That would have taken too long, and my clothes are dirty. Also, I'm hungry." She went over to inspect the tray. "So did you get stuck with Diana duty today? Let me guess. Tormod is tired of trying to keep up when I do my five miles."

"Why do you run so?" he couldn't help asking.

"You don't have a treadmill." She took a sip of the tea and grimaced. "Hot herb and honey water again. Terrific. You guys really haven't discovered coffee yet?"

"Kinley says it will be another two hundred and fifty years before it reaches Britannia." He watched her sample the oatcake, and imagined feeling her pretty mouth on his skin until he felt a hard, thin heat spread along his jaw. Why did she rouse his battle spirit? "This coffee must be a wondrous drink."

"Mmmm, no. It's kind of like bitter, liquid dirt. It's the caffeine kick I miss." She glanced at him. "We're a little strange in the future. So what made you ink your face like that?"

"'Twas the custom when I was a lad," Raen said. Since he couldn't explain to her just how long ago that was, he nodded toward the two large grain sacks sitting by the wall. "What do you with those?"

"Weight lifting. It's a form of exercise. Most women in my time don't sit around and embroider cushions." She pulled up another chair to the table where she ate. "Sit down. Have an apple or an oat…cookie?"

"Cake," Raen said and joined her. He drew his eating knife to cut slices from the apple. "You seem so easy now, being here. Kinley didnae trust anyone at first."

Diana moved her shoulders. "I'm a cop. We never trust anyone. But Kinley is healthy, seems happy, and has married a good guy with a castle and lots of stuff. The island is beautiful. I'm stuck in the tower of solitude here, but you do let me out to exercise. Really, aside from the absence of coffee and plumbing and basic human rights, what's not to like?"

He didn't know what to say. "I brought you food."

Diana laughed. "Yes, you did. Sorry. I might be going a little stir-crazy."

"Have you no husband or children to miss you? Family?" When she shook her head Raen felt an odd surge of relief, and then recalled that Kinley, too, had been alone in her time. "But you had friends."

"Friends at work, sure." Her mouth twisted. "Not a lot of time for socializing when you work missing persons. You always think if you try a little harder, and put in more hours, you'll find them." Her gaze grew distant. "Kinley was—is— my last case. It's good to go out on a win."

He didn't understand what she meant, but her tone sounded bleak.

"Where will you go when you return?"

"Nowhere fast." She stood and picked up the outer garments she had shed. "I need to wash my stuff, and that lye soap and the little bowl of water the maids give me isn't going to cut it. Do you have a laundry or something?"

"We've a laundress and a wash house." Raen had already anticipated that Diana would be as obsessed with cleanliness as Kinley was, but he felt puzzled by her sudden change of mood. He got to his feet. "Give your clothes to me, and I'll see them cleaned."

"I don't have anything to change into." She

glanced down at herself and frowned. "I could wear your plaid, I guess."

She reached under it and removed the too-small breast band. Raen spun on his heel to give her his back.

"You cannae walk through the stronghold wearing only my tartan, my lady. 'Twould cause the clansmen to, ah, become very agitated."

"Glad to know I can still agitate someone, but I'm not a lady." She walked in front of him, his tartan now wound and folded around her body and shoulders. "Underwear," she said, pointing to the garments. "The top is called a bra, and the bottom are panties. I'm going to need more, and another change of clothes, unless you're willing to part with the plaid."

He would have looked away again, but to be this close and see his tartan clinging to her so lovingly made his blood run fast and hot.

"Our women dinnae wear such...things."

"Even if she was my size, I'll bet the captain didn't pack any extras." She rubbed a fold of the fabric covering her shoulder. "You know, I used to make my clothes in college to save money. I'd mostly tailor guy stuff I bought at Goodwill."

"Garments can be made for you." In this, at

least he could help her. "We have a seamstress at the stronghold."

"No, thanks. I'd rather not go the way of the gown and wimple." Diana gave him a measuring look. "You're the only guy besides the laird who's on my body scale. Can you spare an old shirt and pants?"

Raen thought of his limited wardrobe, most of which was leather or wool, which would chafe her fine skin. "I had a semat and trews made for the laird's wedding. I willnae wear them again."

"Perfect," she said, and bundled her clothing. "Let's go see the seamstress before we hit the wash house. I'm going to need some things."

Raen took her through the back halls to the sewing rooms, where the castle's seamstress grudgingly supplied Diana with needles, pins, thread and shears from her mending basket. From there they went out to the washing house, where the laundress and the chamber maids were busy boiling and beating the day's laundry. The smell of the lye and tallow being used to clean the linens wafted over them as the red-faced, sweaty laundress looked up from her labors

"If Meg Talley thinks to send back the aprons to be washed again, Seneschal," the laundress said, "I'll put a bat to her arse. They're as clean as they're getting." She regarded Diana. "If she's to work here, she'll no' do it wrapped in a plaid."

"That's okay." Diana coughed a little as she took in the great washing caldrons, bucking vats and wooden bats. "I can do my own laundry." She peered at a basin of soft brown soap. "But not with that goop."

"I've something gentler," Raen told her, and led her back into the stronghold, where he took her to his new rooms in the upper hall.

"This is different," Diana said as she walked around his study. "Did you raid a church, or are you just into dark and depressing?"

"Everything belonged to Evander, the seneschal before me." He had done nothing to change the sparsely-furnished study and bedchamber, to which Evander Talorc's gloomy austerity still seemed to cling. It had suited Raen's own mood since being named the new seneschal. "I come here only to sleep."

"I'm not a nester either," she admitted. "I pretty much live at work, or in my Caddy. That's my car. It's what we use instead of horses to get around in the future."

"Kinley has told us of the machines from your time," Raen said but heard the loneliness in her voice. What idiots the men of the future were, that they had not claimed Diana for their own. He went to the trunk where his predecessor had left behind some fancy goods he'd bought on the mainland, and took out a small, carved wooden box. "Here."

She took the box and opened the lid to examine the small, pale cakes inside.

"'Tis fine soap, made from oils and scented with rose petals," he explained. "The trade ships bring it in from Hispania."

Diana took out one cake and sniffed it. "Nice. Evander leave this behind, too?" When he nodded she smiled. "He must have smelled pretty."

"Evander likely bought it for Fiona, his lover. He ran away with her."

Raen resisted the urge to touch his throat and went into the bedchamber to retrieve the wedding garments.

"You didn't like this Evander guy, I take it," Diana said. She had followed him in and now sat on the end of his bed. "I'd feel the same way if someone tried to kill me."

He stopped sorting through his garment trunk and stared at her.

"Who told you that?"

"Confidential informant," she said and nodded at his hand. "You rub the back of your neck like that every time someone mentions Evander Talorc, too. So what happened?"

"I caught Evander fleeing Dun Aran with his mortal mistress, Fiona, who was spying on the clan for the undead." He couldn't tell Diana that Evander had thrown a spear that had rammed through his neck and nearly severed his spine. She would wonder how he had survived such a ghastly injury. "He attacked me and left me for dead, but the laird and his lady found me in time."

Diana grimaced. "You were very lucky."

"Aye." He wanted to tell her that luck had nothing to do with it. That if not for Kinley, and the magic she possessed that allowed him to cross over and back again from her time in order to be healed, Raen would have died. "I am very grateful to them."

She studied his face. "What happened to Evander and Fiona?"

He shrugged. "No one has seen them since

that day. If they return, Evander knows they will both be put to death for betraying the clan."

Even so, Raen hoped that they wouldn't. He had enough of love's blood on his hands.

Diana frowned and looked around the room.

"So why are you keeping all of Evander's stuff? Guy tried to kill you."

"I only sleep here." He brought the linen garments to her, and watched her lift them to her face. "You can wash them, but I wore them only once."

"They smell like you." She stood up, and suddenly only a few inches separated them. "Thanks for letting me have them."

"You need clothes," Raen said and glanced down to see a lock of her gilded copper hair clinging to his tunic. He gently removed it as an excuse to touch the soft, fine strands. "You should wear a head veil."

"Not even if you drugged me, Big Man." Her eyes widened, and she touched his hot cheek. "Your ink. It's turning white."

"'Tis the lightning spirit in me." He pressed her palm against his skinwork to let her feel the heat. "'Tis what permits me to move so quickly. I dinnae ken why, but you call to it, Diana."

"It feels like it's moving." She trailed her fingers down to his jaw before she suddenly snatched her hand from his and shook it. "Ouch. It bites."

Raen saw the tiny, jagged mark on her upturned palm, and knew exactly what it was. But why this woman? And why now?

"Why did it jump on me?" Diana asked, echoing his confusion as she rubbed the spot. "And what kind of ink do you guys use?"

He wanted Diana, but he could not have her. Raen knew that. Once she felt satisfied that Kinley was being well-treated she would return to her own time. He could not follow her there. Even if he could convince her to stay, his heart still belonged to his dead wife.

"It will go away," he lied to her, and placed the clothes back in her hands. "I will take you back to your rooms now."

Chapter Eight

❧

S PENDING MOST OF the afternoon washing her clothes and tailoring Raen's to fit her leaner frame gave Diana plenty of time to think. Now and then she would check her palm. The little jag of ink that had jumped from Raen's face to her skin no longer felt hot. Though it didn't hurt, she'd tried to scrub it off, with no luck. After a lifetime of not believing in magic Diana had to deal with getting thrown back in time eight hundred years and being stabbed or bitten by Raen's facial tat. Worse, every time she thought of the big man, her little jag tingled like a schoolgirl about to get her first kiss.

When they'd been standing a couple of heart-beats away from each other, the big man had wanted to kiss her. Diana would have bet a paycheck on it. So why hadn't he?

Tormod brought in a tray for her close to sunset, which he thumped down on her side table as he scowled at her. As she cocked an eyebrow at him, he folded his scarred, tattooed arms.

"I am a map-maker, Red, no' a maid."

"I never requested room service," Diana said. She stood and turned in a three-sixty to show him her new outfit. "What do you think? Doesn't it scream medieval chic?"

"Clothes have no mouths and cannae scream, and dinnae tell me they do in your time. I will have nightmares." He inspected her and added gruffly, "You sew well enough for such a mannish wench. I've trews that need mending, if you want more work."

"After sitting in here all day I'm more in the mood for another run." Diana laughed at his alarmed expression. "I'm kidding. How about we go hang with the other highlanders?" She headed for the door.

"Hang from what?" the Norseman demanded as he followed her out to the stairs.

Down in the great hall several dozen clansmen were seated around the trestle tables and talking while they carved, sharpened knives, mended various things and drank. In one corner Diana spotted a gang of men surrounding two who were playing what looked like checkers. All of the men stopped talking as soon as she came into view.

"Hi," she said and put on her brightest smile. "And before you ask, fack, yes, I'm another one."

One short, brutally-muscled man playing the checkers game got up to peer at her. "Be watchful, lads. 'Tis the outsider wench who makes holes in old, helpless magic folk."

"Not deliberately," she countered. As the short, stocky man approached her Diana noted the huge hammers inked on his arms, and the men gathering like a small army behind him. "And you are?"

"He is our sword master and armorer, Neacal, Chieftain of the Uthar tribe," Tormod said quickly. "Chieftain, meet Lieutenant Diana Burke of the San Diego Missing Police Unit." He frowned. "Or some such unit."

"A too-tall wench with a too-long name," the chieftain said. His biceps bulged as large as watermelons as he propped his fists on his hips, and stopped just far enough away not to have to look up at her. "Take her back to her room, Viking."

"Didn't the laird tell you?" she asked. "I'm not a prisoner." She strolled past him and went to the gaming table to study the board. "This is checkers, right?"

"Draughts," Tormod muttered as he caught up with her. "We can go for another run before the sun sets, Red. Come along now."

"Tomorrow." Diana watched Neacal, who stomped over to the other side of the table. "Want to play me, Chief?"

"Chieftain," he corrected her. "And no. I dinnae play with wenches." As his men chuckled he silenced them with a glare. "Females cannae call out men."

"Come on, one game. If you win, I'll go back and stay in my room," she offered. "If I win, you let me hang—ah, stay here and get to know you and the clan."

Neac glanced around at the men, all of whom were looking at the walls and vaulted ceiling.

He dropped onto the bench seat. "Black or white?"

Diana sat down. "White." She watched as one of his men poured a measure of whiskey into two tankards. "What's with the drinks?"

"You lose a counter, you drink," Neac said

and gave her an evil grin. "First one to lose all moves or fall down drunk loses."

The game lasted all of ten minutes. Neac formed a defensive pyramid of counters but neglected to preserve his back row. Diana advanced by taking two counters for each one she sacrificed until she reduced his numbers. The chieftain's tankard had to be refilled seven times, and by the time she crowned her first of three kings he was swaying on his bench.

Taking all of his pieces would have been a little mean, so Diana simply blocked in his remaining counters and met his gaze.

"You're out of moves, Chief."

The clansmen around them murmured and shifted positions to peer at the board.

"I've one more." He raised one of his huge fists, only to open it and offer it to her. "I yield, wench. Woman. Lieutenant?"

"Diana," she said and caught his hand. Though she half-expected him to crush her fingers, all she received was a wobbly shake. "Good game, Neacal."

"Neac." When she would have drawn her hand away he caught her wrist, and turned her palm up to frown at the small gray jag of ink. He turned it over again, and bellowed at Tormod, "Where is Raen Aber?"

The Norseman shrugged. "He's no' had her, if that's prodding your spleen."

"I'll use my spleen to beat some sense in that lad if he'll no' honor his spirit," Neac told her as he stood on unsteady legs. "Bring her, Viking."

Tormod glanced at Diana. "Best we go with him until he falls down."

The chieftain didn't collapse, but lumbered out of the hall and through a back corridor that opened into a lush herb and flower garden. There Diana saw Raen talking with the younger druid, Cailean Lusk.

"Seneschal, a word," Neac shouted as he staggered toward Raen. "Now. Viking, come here so I dinnae kill him."

"Lieutenant Burke," the young druid said. He came over and bowed to her, although he didn't seem especially happy to see her. "I hope you are enjoying your visit."

"Sure. I haven't shot anyone else, either." She glanced over at the three other men. "So how is the old guy?"

"If you mean Master Flen, his wound is slowly healing." Cailean tucked his long, pale hands into the ends of his flowing sleeves. "You must miss your life in San Diego. The laird's wife has told us that it is a marvelous city."

"I bet you'd love the Central Library," she told him as she watched Neac making some cutting gestures, and Raen's expression darkening. "Nine stories of glass and concrete, six million books, and pretty much all the pretty co-eds you can chase. Why do Raen and Neac look like they're about to fight?"

"They are Pritani. 'Tis their nature." His soft eyes shifted to her face. "You have seen that Lady McDonnel is well-treated here. If you are ready to go back, I can help you return to your time. Tonight, if you wish it."

"Everyone wants to get rid of me," Diana said as she watched Neac take a swing at Raen, miss, and fall to the ground. Tormod helped the big man pick up the chieftain's sagging body and carry him into the stronghold. "Why is that?"

"I cannae tell you," Cailean said and gestured at a path that led out of the garden. "Shall we walk down to the loch? 'Tis beautiful when the moon rises."

She wondered why he wanted her by the water, and decided to find out. "Sure."

Walking through the grass to the embankment stirred up a swarm of fireflies, many of which crawled up to perch on Cailean's shoulders. The little bugs formed glittering epaulets as the druid pointed out some of the oldest trees surrounding the loch, including one giant oak that shaded two old, upright stones.

"The trees are very pretty," she said. "They're your thing, right? Wood magic or something?"

Cailean chuckled. "All trees contain great magic. Did you never feel that when you were a wee lass?"

"I haven't been considered wee since the third grade." She stopped and turned to him. "I don't feel magic, either. I do feel annoyed, especially when you hustle me off so you can say things you don't want the clan to hear."

"Druids are by nature very private people," Cailean said, and studied her face for a moment. "I wish only to ask you some questions about matters important to us. May I?"

Diana had the feeling he felt a little afraid of her, and knew she could use that to get some answers out of him. But she was tired of playing bad cop.

"If you'll do the same for me, sure." She sat

down on the ground and stretched out her legs. "Ask away."

He lowered himself down beside her. "Is there anything you can do that 'tis…unusual?"

Diana thought for a moment. "I'm very good at yoga. I can wiggle my ears, and solve crossword puzzles without cheating. I can't sing but I can whistle anything, including most bird calls."

"This would be a powerful talent. Something you hide from others." As she frowned at him he added, "'Tis a sign you have druid blood. In our first incarnation, as you are now, we discover our magic. It will be an ability that others in your time dinnae have."

She thought of the sparkling trail that had led her to the castle, and smiled broadly.

"Sorry. I'm the most non-magical person I know."

"Your power may have come to you in childhood," he persisted. "If it frightened you, you could have locked it away inside yourself."

"I spent a lot of time as a kid locked up," Diana said. "But not by magic."

She looked out at the moonlit water, and imagined tossing the druid into it for reminding her of those bad old days.

"Were you troubled?" he asked.

"I was too big," she said and glanced at him. "By the time I was twelve I was six feet tall, and being my size is not a plus in foster care. It costs more to feed someone like me. The people who were paid to take care of me generally liked to keep all that money for themselves, so they starved me. When I got so desperate I tried to steal food, they beat me and locked me up. By the time my case worker noticed during an unannounced visit, my hair had started falling out, and I had a nasty case of rickets. My bones had grown so soft they found five unhealed fractures leftover from the beatings."

Cailean looked stunned. "'Tis how they treat children in your time?"

"Unwanted kids, yeah, sometimes. My mother killed herself when I was a kid, so they gave me to those people. But I was lucky, too. Once she knew I was being abused, my case worker got me medical treatment, and then put me in a group home, where things were better. Not that it lasted." She shrugged. "It never does. All right, my turn." She faced him and held up her marked palm. "I got this when I touched the tattoos on Raen's face. What does it mean?"

He blinked. "Naught that I ken."

"You're lying to a cop," Diana warned him. "That's about as smart as dangling raw meat in front of a hungry wolf. Also, I told you the truth, and if you don't do the same that makes you a welcher. It's not a good thing. Just tell me."

"Master Aber's tribe used skinwork to offer themselves to certain spirits. If the spirit favored the man, it bonded with his markings, and slumbers inside him until needed." Cailean nodded at the mark. "That spirit woke up when you touched him, and it chose you. Such things were very rare even in…the past."

Now she felt even more confused. "What did it choose me for?"

"Master Aber," the druid said. "It marked you as his mate. It chose you to become his wife."

Chapter Nine

TWILIGHT'S ROYAL COLORS surrounded the druid settlement, adding a dark cloak to the enchantment that had kept it concealed from mortal eyes for ten centuries. Tall, staked torches flared to life with spellfire to illuminate the paths winding around the simple dwellings. A pair of druid children stood counting livestock returning from the pastures, and watched the bespelled creatures nudge open gates and pen themselves for the night. Others returning from wild herb collecting stopped to trade some of their fragrant bunches for vegetables from those who worked in the food gardens.

Each druid who passed one particular home touched a branch of the pear tree that shaded the entry. The traces of magic they left behind sank into the fruit and turned them golden and sweet, as a gift for the old soul who had returned from the outside world wounded and troubled.

In his bed chamber Bhaltair Flen did not smell the ripening pears, or hear the murmured well wishes. He huddled under his coverlet, his eyes moving rapidly beneath his eyelids. In his mind he was again in his first life. He had been sent to perform a cleansing ritual after a plague, and had lost his heart to a young mortal beauty orphaned by the sickness. It had been such a gentle thing, that love, and yet it had consumed him. He had not returned to his settlement, but lingered, to be with her.

In his dream, as it had been in his first life, it did not end well. When the tribe's chieftain had betrothed Yana to a brutish ally, Bhaltair had challenged the match. He had expected to discuss the matter reasonably, not be beaten nearly to death.

Yana is to be my wife, you wand-waving fool. The dark, handsome face of Oron Tanse twisted with a sneer as he raised his bloody knuckles. *She carries my name and my child.*

As the fist came down for another blow the

old druid jerked awake. It took a moment to realize that he lay safe in his bed. He had been disgraced and nearly died of Oron's beating, but in the end vengeance had been his. Yana and her savage husband had died as mortals, never to live again as Bhaltair did. No one even remembered their names anymore.

His heart thudded dully as he offered the gods a short prayer of gratitude. Yet the calm that should have come to him brought instead the memory of Yana's sweet eyes, swimming with tears, and the soft sound of her voice begging him to understand the unfathomable.

Forgive me. I cannae stay with you. I am with child now.

Without thinking Bhaltair raised his hand to wipe the dampness from his own face. A sharp bolt of pain raced up into his shoulder and neck, making him yelp like an undisciplined boy.

"Master Flen." One of the druidesses who had been caring for him hurried over to the bed, and looked all over him. "Does something ail you? What may I do?"

"Naught. I will manage." He glanced at the window, and when he saw the sun had set he pushed back the linens and swung his legs over to rise from the bed. "Has the conclave assembled yet?"

"Soon," she said and wrapped him in a soft, thin robe. "They now await the laird and his lady." She hesitated before she added, "You shouldnae go yourself, Master. You are still very weak."

"Aye, and the fate of the one responsible is being decided," he said, sitting back down on the bed and extending one leg. "Put on my boots, Sister. I'll no' ignore my duty for my own comfort tonight."

Bhaltair had the druidess fetch his cane for him, but did nothing more to tidy his appearance. He also hobbled slowly through the settlement, and for once allowed his discomfort to show on his face. By the time he reached the meeting house his breathing had grown labored and sweat dampened his silver hair.

"Master Bhaltair," Eangus Gragor said. He had once been Bhaltair's acolyte and rushed to his side. "I'll send for a chair."

"No," he said and gripped his former student's arm, leaning on him. "Help me inside. I must speak before the conclave."

The air inside the house smelled of fresh

herbs and rushes, and a trace of cool, clear water. The latter Bhaltair recognized as belonging to the McDonnel laird, Lachlan, whom he saw standing with some of the elder conclavists. Beside him Kinley Chandler, dressed for once as a female, turned her head and saw him. She leaned close to say something to the laird, and they both came directly to Bhaltair.

"Master Flen," Lachlan said and put a hand on his good shoulder as if to brace him. "How do you fare?"

"Poorly, my lord, poorly." He didn't have to feign the grimace as his knees shook under his robe. "Lady Kinley, 'tis good to see you. Eangus, I would welcome that chair now."

The men guided him over to one of the cushioned chairs by the hearth, and once Bhaltair eased into it Lachlan removed his tartan and tucked it around him.

"You make an old man grateful." He glanced at Kinley, who was pressing her lips together. "Never worry, Lady. In time all 'twill be mended." He cleared his throat before he asked, "Would there be a cup of wine about? It dulls the agony to a tolerable level."

Eangus and Lachlan went off in search of wine, while Kinley sat on a tuffet beside Bhaltair. "Cailean sends his regards, and this." She handed him a small scroll.

"You make a fetching dove, my lady." He let her see his hand tremble as he tucked it in his sleeve. "Has my attacker harmed anyone more?"

"No, and the lieutenant didn't attack you," Kinley said firmly. "It was a terrible accident, Master Flen."

"Mayhap," he said but refused to think about how the outsider woman's violet eyes had flared with alarm as her weapon skewered his flesh. He had come so close to retaliating and striking her dead it still made him feel sick. "The matter will be decided by my brothers and sisters."

Druids rarely gathered indoors as a group, but on the rare occasions they did every window and entry were draped with greenery and left open. The meeting house contained one central, empty room reserved for hearings. When the offense proved grave enough, the oldest and most powerful conclavists among druid kind were summoned to preside over and resolve the matter.

The men returned with a goblet of bell

heather ale, but the dusky purple color of it made Bhaltair's stomach clench. Would everything remind him of Yana now? It was as if the outsider woman had set a memory curse on him.

"I feel much improved," he told Lachlan, and allowed the laird to help him to his feet. In a lower voice he asked, "You've explained the way of this to your lady?"

Lachlan nodded. "Kinley asks only to stand for the lieutenant."

Bhaltair felt no great concern over that. While the lady had druid blood she held no official rank.

"And you, Lord," Bhaltair said. "How do you mean to speak?"

The laird's mouth hitched. "As I ever do, Master Flen."

Inside the meeting chamber the conclave stood in a broad circle around a sickle cast from pure gold that lay upon a slab of polished, marbled green topaz. The ancient tool had once been used by the first druids to collect sacred mistletoe, which had been worked on the slab. Both had been carefully preserved and protected through countless generations and incarnations as a reminder of power and responsibility.

One of the eldest conclavists, chosen by lot

before the gathering as the arbitrator, stepped up to the sickle and slab. He bowed in respect before raising his hands and turning until he had looked upon every face within the chamber.

"We come together in the eyes of the gods," he intoned, "to gather truth and bestow justness. Who brings this matter before the conclave?"

Bhaltair stepped into the circle. "I do. I was wounded by a female outsider who crossed over in the sacred grove on Skye. She is druid kind, or she would no' have opened the time portal." He waited until the murmurs stopped before he continued. "This outsider entered Dun Aran and attacked Seneschal Tharaen Aber there. I challenged her by word alone, and she replied with great contempt. When I didnae yield, the weapon she brought with her blasted a hole through my arm." He opened his robe and tugged down the bandage to expose the wound. "Here is the proof."

A few of the conclavists stepped closer to examine Bhaltair's arm, and then conferred in low voices. Finally they returned to the circle as the arbitrator asked, "Who speaks for the accused?"

"I do." Kinley came to stand beside Bhaltair.

"Diana Burke is an officer of the law in my time. She was searching for me when she fell into the grove portal. She didn't know what had happened to her, or where she was. She reacted as she would have in our time. But she did not deliberately injure Master Flen."

The conclavists asked questions about Diana, the nature of her weapon, and her knowledge of druid kind. Bhaltair listened closely to everything the laird and his lady said about the outsider, but they knew little of her, and offered no valid reason to keep the woman at Dun Aran.

But Bhaltair knew exactly who she was. He had known it the moment he had looked into her flowery eyes.

She will be made to go back, or I will send her there myself.

"Master Flen," the arbitrator said, making him flinch. "Do you wish to speak on the lady's claims?"

He inclined his head, and bowed politely to Kinley before he spoke to Lachlan. "The conclave respects you and your clan, my lord, as friends and protectors of the druids. But you are not druid kind. Unhappily, this outsider woman is." He regarded the faces of his brothers and sisters.

"Only druid blood could have allowed this female to come to our time. As a druidess born she may possess more power, even greater than the weapon used to hurt me."

"Or she may no'," the laird countered. "We dinnae ken the nature of druid kind from her time."

"What we ken is that she isnae aware of it. She has no previous incarnation to guide her. I am sorry to say 'tis no' your concern, my lord." Bhaltair held up his hands. "Forget the pain I suffer, brothers and sisters, and think on what an untrained druidess could do." He nodded at Kinley. "What we have already seen done."

The laird's wife gave him a narrow look. "You mean, like save the lives of all the druids in this settlement from the undead? Do you remember how I did that, Master Flen? I burned to death for you."

"So you did, my lady. 'Twas why we brought you back, and gave you the gift of immortal life." Bhaltair regarded the arbitrator. "I have shown good cause to consider this outsider female too reckless and dangerous to remain among us. I ask nothing for myself in this matter. I but call on the conclave to see her returned to her time."

The arbitrator lifted the golden sickle from its slab and held it aloft. Slowly he turned, slicing the blade through the air until he had passed it before all assembled. Gently he replaced it and bowed before he stepped back.

"What does that mean?" Bhaltair heard Kinley whisper.

"They have cast their votes on the matter," Lachlan murmured. "Watch now."

The sickle's blade grew bright, and long vines of mistletoe appeared above the gathered druids. The sacred plant wove itself into an intricate cable of white and green light as it hovered briefly over Kinley and Lachlan. Finally it floated away from them to Bhaltair, descending over his face to drape his neck before it dimmed and vanished.

Bhaltair's arm throbbed like a rotten tooth, but he could bear it now. That demon-eyed female would be made to leave, and he would never again think on her or Yana or anything that put holes in him.

"The conclave finds for Master Flen," the arbitrator said to the laird and his lady. "We agree that Diana Burke will be sent back."

Lachlan nodded. "I am grateful for your wisdom, but I believe that Lieutenant Burke will soon choose to return to her time. There is naught to keep her here."

"My lord," Bhaltair said as his jaw sagged. "Has she no' done enough harm? You cannae wait. She must be taken to the grove as soon as you return to Skye. The very moment."

The laird's mouth flattened, and then he turned to his wife and spoke quietly with her. Finally he nodded and turned back to the conclave.

"We will consider your counsel and discuss the matter with our clan," the laird said. "Thank you for your guidance."

Without another word he took Kinley's arm and left the chamber.

Bhaltair stared after them, unable to grasp what had just happened, and then turned on the arbitrator.

"But she must go. This night. The conclave decided it."

"Were the wench here, yes," the elder druid said. "But the McDonnels have her and, among the clan, Lachlan has the final word. We cannae storm the castle and take her from them. Mayhap 'twill be as the laird said. The female hasnae reason to remain."

"As you say, Brother," Bhaltair said.

He had been beaten again, but he felt no outrage or pain. The calm he had prayed for filled him like soft, icy snow, for this time he would not accept defeat. This time, he would strike back.

Chapter Ten

RAEN FINISHED CARRYING up the last of the new bales to the hay loft, and came down to find Seoc Talorc glumly repairing tack. Since Evander had run off with his lover the stable master had been spending more and more time alone, and now looked drawn and gaunt, as if he had not been sleeping or eating. As Evander's cousin, Seoc had been shunned by many of their clansmen. Despite all Raen's duties, he had made a point to spend a little time with the stable master when he could.

"'Tis kind of you to help, Seneschal," Seoc said, and put aside the bridle he had mended. "Has there been any word from the laird and lady?"

"Yes, they are spending another night on the mainland." He eyed the worn saddle the stable master had mounted on his stitching form. "Why do you mend that? 'Tis older than the clan."

"'Tis fitted for Tormod Liefson's bony arse," Seoc said. "He'll no' have another until the wood rots away from under him." He frowned at the saddle. "I promised him he could fit the new hide at today noon, when his guard duty ended."

Raen winced. "I go to relieve him now." He disliked meddling, but added, "Leave the saddle, and come up to the hall tonight. The maids have been pining for you."

"These would be the same maids who've been showing their backs to me ever since my cousin turned traitor?" Seoc gave him a doleful look. "You were never a good liar, Raen Aber."

"Aye." He touched the stable master's shoulder. "But you are missed, Brother, and by more than me."

As Raen walked from the stables to the stronghold, he knew he would have to speak to Lachlan about Seoc. The laird was well aware of the man's shame, and a show of trust in Seoc would do much to relieve his silent suffering. He only wished he could do the same for Diana.

Last night, when he'd gone to find her and the druid, he'd overheard everything she'd told Cailean Lusk about her childhood. It appalled him to think of anyone starving and beating a child for simply being hungry, but to know it had been done to the lieutenant enraged him. It also explained why she spent so much time running and lifting and bending herself in impossible shapes. Her strong, lovely body had once been sickly and weak.

Knowing what Diana had suffered had shocked him almost as much as his lightning spirit marking her as his mate—and he had yet to speak to her about the latter. She had told Cailean that she didn't believe in magic, so she would likely scoff at the Pritani of old, and the powers sometimes bestowed on them by their chosen spirits. Diana still remained unaware that the McDonnel clan had been brought back from the dead, and that they had lived as immortals for more than a millennia.

Raen had hoped the laird and his lady would have returned by now, so they could decide what to tell the lieutenant. Instead he would have to guard her another night. Tormod met him at the base of the tower stairs.

"She's gone from her room," the Norseman said and grimaced. "She wanted to see where the river empties into the ocean, but I told her 'twas too late for a walk. 'Twas why she sent me to fetch her bathing water, so she could steal away. A *jötunn* would be easier to keep penned."

"She is bored," Raen said suspecting that Diana had finally grown impatient with her confinement. "I'll bring her back and watch her for the night. Go and get some sleep."

"You'll want chains for her," the Norseman predicted. "And mayhap a large cudgel for yourself."

Raen sent a guard to inform Neac he was leaving the stronghold, and took the path through the ridge peaks that led down to the river. Tormod's solution to every problem with females involved fetters and raiding tactics, but if he could not convince Diana to cooperate, Raen might very well have to put her in shackles.

As he reached the edge of the estuary, he saw a torch that had been wedged upright between two large rocks beside Diana's shoes. He stared at the odd footwear, for they made no sense to him. Why would she remove them here, unless…

"Diana." He rushed to the edge of the water, yanking off his boots and vest as he peered out at the dark, cold waters. "Where are you? Call to me."

He heard a splash as he stripped out of his trews, and looked over to see a pale figure sinking beneath the surface. He waded in and dove deep, dissolving into his water-bonded form that made him as fast as light. He streaked through the murky depths until he felt the warmth of her, and surfaced.

Several yards away Diana did the same, gasping as she wiped a hand over her face.

"Boy, I'm glad I grew up by the Pacific. This water makes frigid sound cozy."

Raen changed back and swam over to her, only to see her submerge and dart beneath him. He spun, blinking the sting of salt from his eyes until he saw her again.

"You can *swim?*"

"You thought I couldn't?" she said as her lips curved. "Aw, you jumped in to save me? That's adorable. I should mention that I was a real jock in college. I lettered in distance swimming, softball and track."

"I thought you were drowning!" That he shouted the words made him feel even more the fool. He clamped down on his temper. "The sea is too cold. You cannae swim here."

"I can't swim, I can't leave the castle, and I can't walk around without a guard." She made a rude sound. "What *can* I do?"

"No' scare me like this. 'Twould be very good to do that." He reached out and pulled her into his arms, and then stiffened the moment her skin brushed his. "Diana, why are you naked?"

"You haven't invented the swimsuit yet. Or the wetsuit, for that matter." She lifted her arms and linked her hands behind his neck. "You're naked, too."

"I was saving you, no' seducing you." He tried to put some space between them, but she curled her long legs around his. "We will sink."

She leaned close to press her cheek against his and whispered, "I don't care."

Raen felt the lightning spirit awakening, and quickly turned his head to break the contact with her skin.

"I ken what Cailean told you, but you are no' my wife. You dinnae belong here. 'Tis a mistake."

"Doesn't feel like one at the moment," she said but drew back a little. "We're naked and alone, Big Man. We've both wanted this since you tied me to that bed." She slid her palm up to cover his marked cheek. "Feel it? It's like you're already inside me."

Raen clamped her against him and swam one-armed until he could touch bottom. Then he trudged out of the water. When he set her on her feet her breasts grazed his chest, and the soft curls of her sex clung to the throbbing base of his erection. He would do the decent thing and set her away from him, as soon as he had warmed her, as soon as she stopped touching him, as soon as the spirit subsided—

He dragged her up against him, glorying in the feel of her resilient, slender form as he kissed her. Her lips parted for him, and he ravished her mouth, the way he had wanted to since the night she had come to the castle. His hands found their way down to her buttocks, and he clasped the firm curves, pressing her against his throbbing cock and rubbing her against his shaft. She made a small, sweet sound and hitched herself up on him, her breasts dragging against his chest as she grabbed a handful of his hair. He wanted to fack her so badly he shook with it, but he wrenched his mouth from hers.

"Diana, we mustnae…"

"Please find a place where we can stretch out," she said, sounding breathless and eager. "Grass, rock, glen, I don't care. I need you." She moved against him, letting him feel the slickness of her little quim. "See? You know you want it, and God, so do I."

"We cannae," he said, as he set her down and backed away from her. "I am no' for you. I cannae have you."

"You can have me right now," she assured him. "I'm right here, I'm naked, I'm willing. Is there something else I need to do or say?"

Bright, hot power began to spark inside him.

"Please," he said through clenched teeth. "Go back to the castle. Now. Hurry."

It was too late to stop it. He knew it as soon as he felt his face burn. The chilly air crackled around them as his ink came alive and spilled down over his heart, spattering her with its silver-white sparks of power.

"Oh, my god," Diana gasped and covered the

flow with her hands as if to stop it. "What is happening to you?"

"It's awake now," Raen said tightly as he wrapped his arms around her, pressing her long, lovely body against his. "Be still, or the spirit will take what it wants from us."

DIANA WATCHED the ink spread across Raen's chest in a glittering web.

"It? You mean your tattoos? They're alive?"

"The spirit inside them," he muttered. "Ah, fack."

"Tattoos don't light up and move around. They can't." She could feel it moving under her fingers. "But yours do. What does this spirit want exactly?"

"You." The light crackling across his skin echoed in tiny white glints in his gray eyes as he glanced down. "'Tis my longing for you it shares. It wants you."

His ink spilled from his chest onto her breasts, and spun around Diana's beaded, puckered nipples. The hot, sparkling sensation radiated into her chest and belly. It was absolutely sexual as the ink tightened on her peaks and trickled down toward her thighs.

"I think your tattoos are feeling me up." Her breasts ached so much she pressed them against his unyielding muscles, which provided a little relief. "Shouldn't it, I don't know, kiss me first?"

Raen caught her chin between his thumb and fingers and tilted her face up as he bent his head.

"Your lips are mine, Diana. I willnae share them."

His mouth might have looked hard, but when it covered her lips it felt just as luscious and sexy as the first time he'd kissed her. The way he went at it, all desperate and hungry, made her shiver with delight. She opened for him, and he took her with his tongue, tasting and stroking her with frank, carnal greed. No man had ever kissed her the way she really wanted it—not until tonight. He kissed her as if she were precious and fragile, and also as if he were having sex with her mouth, all at once.

"No," she muttered when he took his mouth away. "Don't go all polite and remote on me now. Do that again."

"'Tis too dangerous, my lady." Raen cradled the back of her head with his hand, and pressed her cheek against his chest. Like her he was panting, and under her clutching hands his tough muscles felt more like rock than flesh. "We are strangers still. I cannae lay claim to you, no' when you are to return to your time."

"Maybe I'll stay and claim you." She felt something like a tingling lick over her clit, and groaned. "I think the spirit just voted for that."

Raen muttered something in a strange language, and picked her up as if she were a doll. He carried her to a patch of thick grass, knelt, and lowered her onto her side. But then he lay down behind her, stretching one massive arm across her waist.

"If we dinnae feed its longing, 'twill return to me and sleep again." He sounded a little desperate. "Tell me of your time. Kinley says you have castles and towers of glass in your city."

"I guess we do," Diana said, and pillowed her head on her arm. But it wasn't the city she thought of. Instead she relished the powerful heat of his body which, along with the ink streaking over her skin, seemed to wrap every inch of her in soft warmth. "San Diego has a big harbor, with lots of boats and yachts and ships. I like to watch them coming into dock." She glanced down at the ink scrolling across the insides of her thighs. "This isn't working, and I don't want to talk about home. I don't want to talk at all. I want to violate your body in a hundred different ways."

He took hold of her hand in a way that told her he was trying not to do anything else with it.

"You are not… We both want you too much, my lady."

"I get that," she said and shamelessly pressed her bottom against the thick, hard length of his penis. "Remember what almost happened when you tied me up?"

"Aye." He nuzzled her neck, and shifted her right leg so that her calf rested atop his. "When I tied you to that bed, I didnae wish to leave you. I desired to stay, and open your strange garments, and look upon you naked and beautiful beneath me. I wished it so much my cock turned to iron." His hand released hers, and moved up to cup one throbbing breast. The way he caressed it made Diana swallow a moan. "I couldnae rid myself of that wanting until much later, when I lay in my bed, and thought on you as I rubbed myself."

"That's good," Diana said and took in a quick breath as she felt him press his heavy length between her thighs. "But you should have come back and let me do it. I like playing in bed, and I'd love playing with you."

"I didnae ken you truly wanted me, until I gave you my wedding clothes." He stroked his thumb in a circle around her peak, soothing the tight pucker of her aureole. "Desire makes your eyes darken to amethyst. Or did I see only what I wanted?"

"No, you nailed it. I almost ripped off the tartan." She shifted her hips until her damp, sensitive folds nestled against his shaft. Raen began stroking her with short, easy thrusts, and the ridge of his cockhead grazed her pulsing clit. "Oh, that feels even better than the tats. Maybe, ah, you could do that inside me?"

"You need more, my passionate one, and I shall give it to you," Raen said, his voice taking on an eerie rasp. "Open to me, golden rose, and I shall fill your sweet softness over and again until the joy of it floods you with me."

Diana found herself on her back, with the big man on top of her. His eyes glowed bright silver now as he bent his head to latch onto her breast, and pressed the head of his throbbing cock against her opening. It would be so easy to let him bury that beautiful erection inside her, and pump it in and out until she came all over him. Her hungry, empty pussy silently screamed for her to do it.

But this wasn't Raen. This was some kind of tattoo demon inside him. She didn't understand what it was, or how it could be controlling him, but going along for the ride wasn't an option.

"You can't make him do this," she declared. When he raised his head, she pressed her marked palm against his heart, and felt the power seething inside him. "Let Raen be with me."

He took her mouth with his, and light shattered between them as his ink seemed to burst into a million tiny shards. The rush of power over her skin flung Diana perilously close to the edge of climax, but she held it back and gasped his name into his mouth.

"You," Raen gasped. He lifted his head and looked all over her face, and the strange light in his eyes dimmed. "'Tis me and the storm inside me, and you are what we want—to have you, to be inside you, to pleasure you until you shriek with delight."

A surge of wetness from her pussy crowned his cockhead, and she smiled up at him.

"Then make me scream, Big Man."

Raen's hands shook as he pushed them under her hips, lifting them as he breeched her and sank into her softness. He was so hard and wide that Diana had a moment of doubt. It had been almost forever since the last time she'd welcomed a man between her thighs. Raen slowed his penetration, his muscles coiling and his shaft swelling as he drew out an inch and came back into her, working his cock to stretch her around him.

"Not my first time," she assured him when she saw his expression. "It's just been a while since—" The heated power of his ink slid down between them, and rushed over the juncture of their sexes. Then it jolted through his shaft into her pussy. "It's inside me, it's...oh, my *god*."

"We both fack you now, golden rose," the spirit rasped through Raen, who shuddered over her before he followed the sensation with a deep, powerful thrust. "You are our woman tonight and always."

Diana arched under him as her body reacted to the double penetration. It felt as if there were two shafts inside her: one made of hard, satiny

flesh and the other formed of light she could feel.
When Raen plowed into her, the spirit cock
seemed to dissolve, only to reform as he slid out.
She'd never felt anything so mind-boggling or
erotic, and then he reared up, impaling her on
both the real and the phantom shafts as he lifted
her and stood, supporting her with his hands
clamped on her buttocks.

She linked her hands behind his neck, unsure
of what he meant to do, and uncaring of what it
was. Then a drop of warm water pelted her face,
and she looked up to see dark clouds laced with
lightning spreading directly overhead.

"Dinnae fear," he said, tilting his head back as
the first curtain of rain doused them both. "This
night we are the storm."

With his tremendous strength he lifted her and
then pressed her down, working her pussy on his
shaft as he thrust deeper and faster. The hard
fucking made her breasts bounce and her heart
hammer, while the downpour caressed every inch
of her with wet heat. She could feel his shaft
thickening with every stroke, and her own clit
pounding as if it meant to burst.

"Tharaen," she gasped. She blinked the water
from her eyes and slid her hand into his soaked

mane, urging his face closer to hers. "Kiss me. I want your mouth on mine when I come."

He plunged into her with one final, rough thrust, and then touched his lips to her mouth. As his tongue glided with hers, she tightened around him, feeling the surge of his seed even as her pussy fluttered with the rush of her climax. Then Diana came as she never had, with heat, and light, and wild, screaming ecstasy, the pleasure streaming from her clit to her nipples and spilling from her mouth to his in one enormous burst of delight.

Raen held her plastered against his chest as he shook, his cock jerking inside her as he pumped her full of his cream. As he came with her the seething clouds began stabbing the sea and the beach around them with jagged, white-hot bolts of power, filling the air with sizzling energy.

The big man fell to his knees as he jetted one last time into her, triggering another, softer orgasm that left Diana shaken and limp. Then they were holding each other on the ground, arms and legs entwined, and it was all she could do to simply breathe. She looked up to see the storm dissipating as quickly as it had formed, and weakly lifted her hand to wipe away the drops clinging to her lashes.

"That was… There aren't words for what that was." She glanced at his face, and saw the jagged marks of ink on his cheek, as if she had just imagined the last hour. "I want to meet your tattoo artist."

"You cannae." He withdrew from her, and rolled away to fling an arm over his eyes.

"I was joking. A little." She pushed herself up with unsteady hands to look at him. "Hey. You just made me believe in magic, and I am not a magic-inclined gal. I even talked to your tattoos. I generally don't have conversations with body ink."

"It shouldnae have happened." He turned his head away.

She felt so exasperated she wanted to thump him. "You're alone in that opinion, Big Man. And you wanted it as much as I did. Wait. You mean the spirit getting into the spirit? That was pretty much every sex fantasy I've ever had. On crack." When he frowned at her she chuckled. "That means I loved it. You, the spirit, the way you two cooperate. It was incredible."

"It hasnae ever done that." He sat up and hunched his shoulders. "You ken naught of me, or

I you, and yet we do this as if…" He stopped and shook his head.

"You want to know about me? I don't have relationships because I work too many hours, and I'm taller than most men. Guys in my time don't like that. I have no family, but plenty of baggage. Back home I use my place only to sleep. I serve and protect the people because someone has to, I'm good at it, and hobbies bore me. Also, I take my time going after what I want, but I don't give up. Even when I know it's risky." Diana tucked her arm through his. "Sound familiar?"

His mouth hitched. "We are much the same."

"That, and we just had sex in a lightning storm, and neither of us paid any attention to it." She grinned. "We are the same kind of crazy, pal."

Raen stood up, and helped her to her feet, taking a good hard look at her body while he did. As she walked over to get her clothes Diana stepped down on something sharp and swore.

"Diana." He came at once, scooping her off her feet and placing her atop a flat, smooth rock. "What is it?"

"I think I cut my foot." She grimaced as she

propped her calf on her thigh to get a good look at it. "Oh, yeah. There's blood."

"That we cannae have." Raen retrieved his tunic, tearing off the sleeve and wrapping it around her foot. "You must take care with wounds here."

"I know you guys don't have antiseptic, but a splash of whiskey should kill the germs," she told him. "It's not deep enough to need stitches."

"'Tis the blood that 'tis the danger here," he told her. "The undead can smell spilled blood from miles away, and use any trail of it to track their victims. If they are starved, the scent alone will make them crazed. In that state they will all pursue the injured mortal like a pack of wolves with foam-mouth."

"Or hungry sharks." Diana shuddered. "On second thought, thanks for the bandage."

They both dressed in silence, and Diana handed him the torch as they started back toward the stronghold.

"I'd like to make small talk, but I suck at that," she told him as they crossed the glen. "So can I ask you something that you're probably not going to answer?" When he gave her a wary look, she said, "It's okay. I know there's a lot no one is telling me. I'm planning to interrogate Kinley about it as soon as she gets back from Druidville. This involves you."

The torchlight illuminated his face, which looked as if she'd kicked him somewhere painful.

"I will answer if I can," he said finally.

"Tormod mentioned that you were married once. Actually, I pumped him for information mercilessly, and he caved in." She stopped on the path and faced him. "What happened to your wife?"

His jaw tightened. "I buried her in a meadow where she went to pick flowers. 'Twas Bradana's favorite place."

On one level Diana felt relieved, and on another she felt sick.

"How did she die?"

"She drowned," Raen said and looked up at the stars for a long moment. "I dinnae mean to be short with you. 'Tis yet painful to speak of her."

"I understand that, but there's something else." She nodded at the ridge that concealed the castle. "Does the entire clan live at Dun Aran? They don't have houses of their own in the village or in the mountains, right?"

"Aye," he said, frowning. "What of it?"

"You've got a couple thousand men living at the castle, but the only women there are me, Kinley, and the servants. I've seen no children at all. So where are all the wives and kids?"

He smiled sadly. "We dinnae have families, Diana. The McDonnels cannae marry, or sire children, and...I cannae tell you why."

Chapter Eleven

J UST AFTER DAWN Diana woke alone in her bed, and stared up at the new linen curtains the maids had hung. Her body still ached pleasantly from her wild night with Raen, but as soon as they'd returned to the stronghold he'd walked her to her room and left her to sleep alone. She suspected he needed time to process what had happened between them. She certainly did. But something else was bothering him. Maybe the memory of the wife he had buried in the meadow of flowers, the wife he'd somehow married when the rest of the clan couldn't get hitched.

That he felt guilty about her came through loud and clear, but Diana had also picked up on some anger. Why would he be mad about losing Bradana?

Tormod came in with her breakfast tray as he relieved the guard Raen had left on her door.

"Fair day to you, Red. Tell me you wrenched an ankle when you stole away last night, so I dinnae have to chase you across the glen."

"No sprains, but I stepped on a sharp rock." She lifted and wiggled her bandaged foot for his inspection. "I won't be running anywhere for a couple of days."

"So there *are* gods, and at last they smile upon me." The Norseman gave her the once-over. "Neac said you and our seneschal returned sodding wet and looking as if you'd tussled."

"It rained. We tussled." She tossed a pear to him from her tray before she took a sip from the steaming mug. "Soothing brew? Seriously? I just woke up."

"Mistress Talley heard of your escape. 'Tis meant to calm you. She imagined you fighting Raen tooth and nail as he dragged you back here." His pale blue gaze shifted to her mouth. "I'll wager you used other parts."

"You have a dirty mind." And amazingly

accurate powers of observation, Diana thought. "Is Raen going to get in trouble?"

He considered that. "If you were unwilling, yes. We're no' permitted to force ourselves on wenches." When he saw how she was looking at him he spread his hands. "'Tis how the Pritani are. I cannae make sense of it. Vikings havenae such rules."

"Yeah, I get that," she said drily. "So when do the laird and lady arrive today? I need to talk to Kinley."

He shrugged and took a bite of the pear. "They will come when they wish." He chewed and swallowed before he added, "We can go down and play draughts while you prop up your foot. You promised to teach me how to crown three in one game."

What Diana really wanted was to go and find Raen, and make sure he wasn't in regret mode over last night, but she knew he started work before dawn.

"If you'll get me some of that spicy brew that clears out my sinuses, it's a deal."

Her cut foot did hurt when she walked downstairs with Tormod, but Diana forgot about the pain as soon as she saw Raen standing and talking with a weathered-looking man in muddy pants and a dripping tartan.

"Who is that guy?" she asked.

"Naught but a courier from the mainland." The Norseman peered at the stranger for a moment. "He wears the Lamont tartan. One of the laird's friends sent him. He travelled by night when he might have sent a bird."

"Does that mean he's got bad news?" she asked, and when he nodded she headed for Raen. When Tormod blocked her path she glared at him. "What if Kinley's in trouble? I'm a cop. It's the job."

"The laird said no speaking with outsiders." He folded his arms. "I'll haul you upstairs and shackle you to the bed post this time, Red. After last night, happily."

Diana eyed the entry to the kitchens, which was just behind where Raen and the man were standing.

"Then let's go get some of that brew I want."

"I will go." He pointed to the draughts table. "You will sit and no' move from that bench until I return." When she started to argue he took her by the arm. "Sit here, or be chained to your bed. It matters no' to me."

She jerked her arm free and stalked over to the bench seat. "You're an ass."

"I'm your guard. 'Tis the job." Tormod gestured to one of the sentries, and pointed at Diana. "Watch her now."

As soon as Tormod went into the kitchens Diana stood, but the sentry stepped forward and shook his head, making her sit back down. Whatever message the Lamont courier had brought had Raen looking bleak. A flutter of flowing robes passed in front of her, blocking her view, and she looked up at Cailean's calm face.

"Fair morning, Lieutenant." He sat down on the other side of the table. "I'm told you went sea-bathing last night. Is that how you injured your foot?"

"No, I kicked a nosy druid into the ocean. It's my new hobby." She craned her neck to see around him, only to discover that Raen and the courier had disappeared. "Damn it. Now how am I going to find out what's wrong?"

"The Lamont clan sent word that the undead have taken the earl's only daughter," Cailean said, startling her. "If the laird and his lady dinnae soon return, Tharaen must lead a warband to the mainland."

Diana knew that the highlanders regularly engaged in undead battles, but the thought of Raen fighting vampires made her stomach knot.

"Why don't the druids do something about it? Can't they cast a cooperation spell over the undead, and make them give up the kid?"

The young druid looked as if she'd kicked him in the teeth.

"Magic isnae a weapon, Lieutenant, and it shouldnae be used as such. The more powerful the spell, the more harm it can do, and it does. It does terrible things."

She had the feeling he was talking about something else.

"Am I in for another truckload of obscure analogies that I'm not going to get because I'm eight hundred years younger than you?"

Cailean's mouth twitched. "I only meant to say that with your talent, you could help him."

Diana stopped watching for Raen. "My what?"

"That power you told me you didnae have." He leaned forward and lowered his voice to a low murmur. "That night you came to Dun Aran, did you feel the clan's presence, or did you follow a trail of light?"

That he knew what had happened made lying about it ridiculous.

"I felt Kinley, and then I found the light trail. How did you know?"

"You couldnae see the castle from the glen. You didnae ken 'twas hidden in the ridges. No one told you of it. Yet you came directly, without once losing your way." He drew a line with his finger from her side of the table to his. "You are a tracker, Lieutenant. 'Tis a powerful talent, and one the seneschal will need if he is to find the missing lass."

Chapter Twelve

WHILE DIANA WAITED at the gaming table, Cailean went to speak with Raen. They returned to the hall with Neac in tow. Tormod came from the kitchen with the brew in his hand and joined them.

"I'll meet with the earl about his missing daughter," Raen said to them. But when Diana opened her mouth, he added. "Alone."

"Alone?" she demanded. "If the undead snatched her, shouldn't you take some of the guys with you as back-up? I mean, help if there's a fight?"

"It couldnae be the legion's work," Raen said, shaking his head. "She vanished from a well-guarded stronghold at midday, when sunlight would have killed any undead."

"'Tis well-known that Lamont dotes on his bairn," Tormod said. "Since he has more coin than the king, 'tis likely his enemies arranged this to ransom her for a pretty price."

Raen nodded his agreement. "I will go and question the servants. One or more may have been bribed to lure her out of the house."

"If they gave her to the undead," Neac said, "send a dove directly, and I'll bring the warband." The chieftain rubbed his big hands together. "'Tis been months since we've made dust out of those blood-suckling bastarts. I cannae wait."

Tormod grunted. "You just want an excuse to use that new double-bladed axe."

"I designed it myself," the chieftain told Diana with obvious pride. "'Twill take a head with one swing, and another when drawn back for the next blow."

"Efficient," she said, concealing a shudder. "Remind me never to pick another fight with you."

"You neednae question anyone, Seneschal, if you but take the lieutenant to Lamont's stronghold," Cailean said, and explained how she'd used her special druid power to find Dun Aran. "Since her talent is new she will need guidance. I am happy to go along with you."

Raen regarded Diana. "You didnae tell me you were a tracker."

"I just found out myself from the druid," she said and pretended to glare at Cailean. "Why didn't you tell me before I was a tracker?"

He cleared his throat. "You, ah, concealed it from me."

Diana turned back to Raen. "So obviously we need to work on our communication skills. We'll make that a priority after we find the missing kid."

Raen didn't look happy. "The laird told me to keep you at the stronghold, Diana."

"The laird's not here, and with my experience I'm your best shot at finding this girl." She suspected he was more worried about her than ignoring the laird's orders. "This is what I do for a living, Raen. At least give me a chance." When he reluctantly nodded she grinned and turned to Tormod. "We'll need a fast boat. Can we borrow one from the village fishermen?"

The Norseman coughed, and Neac gave her a pained smile.

"We dinnae use boats, lass."

Diana tried to wrap her head around what the chieftain told her they did use, all the way until she stood with Raen at the edge of the loch.

"I don't know about this." She pushed back the hood of the dark cloak Neac had given her to wear. "Why can't we go through the sacred grove with Cailean? I've done that already."

"I am no' a druid, and 'tis how the clan travels." He turned her to face him. "You didnae fear my lightning spirit. I want you to see everything I am."

That made her feel a little better. "Okay, but just walk me through this again. You get in the water, and bond with it, and then you…what from there?"

"I travel through it to any other loch, river or stream on the mainland. I have only to think on it, and there I go." He folded his hand over hers. "As long as you hold onto me, so will you."

This water-travel thing was far more intimidating than his over-sexed tattoo. But if she could make love with Raen and his ink, then she could handle this. Maybe.

"Before the clan could pay for stables on the other side," he said, "we trained our mounts to travel with us."

"The horses?" she said, blinking at the mental image.

"'Tis only a matter of gentling them in the water."

She knew what he was doing—and it worked. If horses could do it, so could she.

"I know I told you that I was on the swim team, and I can still hold my breath for a long time." She gripped his hand tightly. "Just not forever. Please don't forget that."

Raen led her into the water until it reached their shoulders, and wove his fingers through hers.

"'Twill be fast. I promise."

Diana nodded, and then went still as Raen ducked under the surface. She did the same, and saw his body shimmer and fade until he looked as if he were made of water. A rush of bubbles engulfed them, and then they were being pulled through the currents.

She could feel and see the loch's dark waters rushing by them, and remembered to hold her breath as she clung to Raen's transparent hand. The weight of the water didn't pull at her or her clothes, and when she tucked her chin in she saw her body had been enveloped by the same light as he radiated. A heartbeat later he was lifting her from the rushing water of a wide, rocky stream and setting her onto the moss-covered bank.

"Wow," Diana gasped and staggered a little. She turned around to see the druid standing just behind her, which made her jump. "Jesus. Will you wear a bell or something?"

"No." Cailean lifted his hands up toward the tree canopy.

A cool wind came out of nowhere and blasted Diana, nearly knocking her on her ass. It stopped an instant later, leaving her standing in a puddle of water. She ran a hand over her tousled hair, which like her clothes and cloak felt only slightly damp now.

"What was that? Your blow dryer talent?" she asked the druid, who shook his head and walked up the embankment. She turned to Raen, who had turned back into his substantial self. "I can't be one of his people. They have no sense of humor."

"You should speak gently to druids," Raen told her, and put an arm around her waist. "Cailean can teach you much, and 'tis no' kind to mock your elder."

"I'll try to be nicer, and thanks for thinking I'm only sixteen, but I've got at least ten years on that boy." She leaned into him, just to be sure he wouldn't disintegrate into a bigger puddle. "How old are you, anyway?"

His jaw tightened for a moment. "Older than you, lass."

"I should have guessed from the gray in your hair. Don't worry. I've always liked older men." She reached up to nuzzle his cheek, and found herself on the receiving end of a brief, passionate kiss. "Do that again and we'll be teaching Junior Druid stuff he's never even imagined."

"You make me forget everything," Raen said. He cupped her cheek, his hand tense, and then sighed. "Come. By now the earl will be frantic."

They caught up with Cailean at the edge of the woods, which bordered a wide, grassy expanse around the base of three high walls made of red stone. Big circular towers stood like oversize rooks at the corners of the castle, while two more slender versions flanked an arched wooden gate. Dozens of dour-faced men wearing the Lamont tartan and carrying drawn long swords stood guard or walked the perimeter in small groups.

"Whoever took the daughter would have had to sneak her out past the guards," Diana said as she noted the drawbridges over not one but two moats. "Maybe some of them were bribed to turn a blind eye to strangers." That reminded her. "How are you going to explain me?"

"I will tell Lamont that you are a druidess to the clan," Raen said. When she would have walked toward the gate tower he tugged her back. 'Twould be better if you dinnae speak, Diana."

"So I dinnae fash Lamont with my strange words and mannish tongue?" Diana said in her best imitation of Meg Talley's brogue, making him grin. "I know, and I'll keep quiet."

The moment they stepped out of the woods, the stronghold's guards rushed over and surrounded them. Each man dropped to one knee and bowed his head, before flanking them and escorting them into the castle.

Diana tried not to gawk, but the earl's fortress was almost as big as Dun Aran, and had been outfitted with the medieval version of luxury décor. Intricately worked tapestries depicting gorgeous landscapes, fantastic creatures and battling high-landers hung on the stone walls above tiled floors. The castle's tall, narrow arched windows had been covered with panels of translucent, oily-looking material that was probably the precursor to glass panes. She could smell something exotic in the wood smoke from the blazing hearths, as if someone had tossed spices into the flames to perfume the air.

The guard brought them into a large receiving room, where a harassed-looking bearded man dressed in furs stood looking up at a portrait of a young girl.

"I told you to leave me be," he said. "Get out."

"My Lord Lamont," Raen said. "We are come from Dun Aran to help find your daughter."

"At last the gods hear me." The earl spun around, his ferocious scowl dissolving as he strode forward to clasp forearms with Raen. "I knew your laird wouldnae deny me help." He took in Diana and Cailean before he frowned. "Where is the warband?"

"I will send for them, once we discover where your lass has been taken." Raen shifted in front of Diana. "These druids will use their magic to track her."

"I dinnae need magic. I need McDonnels." Lamont peered at the big man. "And why would Lachlan send you? You are naught but his bodyguard."

"If you dinnae wish our help, we will go,"

Cailean said before Raen could reply. "And I shall advise the conclave that you have no need of druid kind."

"No, no, wait," the earl said and threw up his big hands, which were shaking. "I mean no disrespect, revered one. Since Nathara was taken I cannae sleep nor eat nor think. Fearing what those craven, cowardly beasts could be doing to my poor, sweet little bairn…" He turned away and uttered a wail of despair.

"'Tis better to leave him to his grief," Cailean told Raen. "We'll have the guards show us where Nathara was last seen. From there the lieutenant should be able to pick up her trail."

"Hang on," Diana said and went over to the earl, who stood rocking himself in front of the painting of a well-dressed adolescent girl with ginger red hair, placid blue eyes and a pouty little mouth. "Is this a portrait of your daughter, my lord?"

"Aye," he said and hardly seemed to notice her as he stared up at the girl's smiling face. "She's the image of her mother, rest her soul."

"She's a beauty," Diana agreed. Though she would have preferred a photograph, she'd work with what medieval times offered. "What was your daughter wearing when she disappeared?"

He dragged a hand over his tear-streaked face. "Her green gown, with her mother's pearls, and a lace veil. Do you ken, those thieving bastarts took all her fine gowns when they stole her from me?"

Taking the victim's nicest clothes was generally not at the top of any kidnapper's to-do list, Diana thought.

"Did anything about Nathara seem different lately? How was she feeling the last time you saw her?"

"She was sad. She told me she loved me." Lamont's whole face screwed up as if he were about to bawl. "'Twas as if she knew we would be parted."

Nathara couldn't have marched past all those guards, but she might have found a way to slip past them, Diana thought.

"Has anything of value other than your daughter's gowns gone missing or been stolen recently?"

"Nathara's maid stole some of her baubles and ran off last week," the earl said and squinted at her. "You're no' Scottish."

"Her people are," Raen said, appearing

beside her. "She is visiting them." He took her arm. "The guards are waiting, Mistress Burke."

As he marched her back over to Cailean, Diana glanced back at the portrait.

"I'm sorry I broke the no-talking promise, but I need to see this girl's room, right now."

❦

TWO GUARDS ESCORTED them up to Nathara's bed chamber, which was in mild disarray. Diana methodically searched every cabinet and trunk, and checked under the feather mattress.

"What do you look for, Lieutenant?" Cailean asked.

"What no one else has noticed."

She climbed onto the bed and stood up to inspect the canopy, and then dropped down and stretched out, rolling her head from side to side.

"Diana, if you are weary, we can rest," Raen said.

"I'm not tired."

She pushed herself off the bed and went over to a large trunk. The floor in front of it showed fresh scrape marks, and a faintly sparkling patch of amber light. With some effort Diana pulled it

out from the wall. The flattened green bundle
stuffed behind it had been tightly folded and tied
with a swath of white lace. The honey-colored
sparkles suffused the fabric.

Raen crouched down beside Diana as she
untied the bundle.

"'Tis the gown Lamont said his daughter was
wearing."

"You get a gold star for paying attention. No
pearls, though. Hmmm." Diana stood and
tossed the green gown onto the bed. "All right.
There's nothing of value in here, and all of the
clothes in the armoire look on the shabby side.
This doesn't jive with a kid who has a rich
daddy that adores her." She drew back the
coverlet from the bed, and looked around the
room. "No basket for the laundress." She looked
at one of the guards. "How tall is Lamont's
daughter?"

The tall man held his hand level with his
midsection.

"Less than five foot even. So she's tiny." Diana
turned to the druid. "I'm not seeing any signs of a
struggle at all. No one could take this kid out of
here against her will. There are just too many
guards. Do you know what that means?"

He looked puzzled. "Mayhap she wasnae taken from this room."

"Or she wasnae taken," Raen said as he looked down at the green gown, and then at the armoire.

When Cailean started to speak she shushed him. "Wait for it."

"But the basket was taken," the big man said and went to the window to look out, and immediately turned around. "The washing house is at the back of the stronghold. That 'twas how it was done."

In that moment he sounded like a cop, and Diana fell a little more in love with him.

"Let's go have a look," she said.

Most of the area behind the castle was used by the servants for laundry, deliveries and outdoor work. It was also not as heavily guarded as the front. The back walls looked too high to climb, and an arch closed off by a heavy iron grate provided the only exit.

Right beside the gate stood the washing house.

As they walked out toward the gate, a cart hauling sacks of flour and grain drew up outside it, where the driver clanged a hanging bell. A man servant came to open the gate, and the wagon drove past the washing house before the driver stopped it by the kitchens to unload.

Raen stopped the man who opened the gate. "Did you work back here on the day the earl's daughter was taken?"

The servant nodded. "Aye, all morning and most of the afternoon."

"What was delivered by cart that day?" Diana asked.

"Ale from the brewery, and firewood from Alick, the forester." He frowned at her. "I ken the drivers both. They've naught to do with this."

Diana peered up at the castle. "Her room is right there. She could see everything from the window." To the servant she said, "Did you see any big baskets in either cart?"

"Alick took one with some mending from the washing house," the man said. "His mother does all of the fine sewing for our lord."

"Why do you care about the basket?" Cailean asked. "'Twas but filled with the lass's gowns and…" The druid's eyes lit up. "Gods, 'twas that how she was taken?"

"Took you long enough," Diana chided. "So now we need to go and talk to Alick the forester."

"I ken his family," Cailean said. "They have a cottage in the brambles beside the silver birch woods, a half-league from here."

Diana went through the gate, and looked around carefully until she spotted the same faint, amber trail she'd seen in the room. It led off down the road and disappeared around the bend. She pointed in that direction.

"Is the cottage that way?" she asked Cailean. When he nodded she smiled at Raen. "Feel like stretching your legs?"

The three of them started down the road, and as Diana watched the trail of light stretching out ahead of them she didn't feel the same tugging sensation that she had on the night she'd come to Dun Aran.

"Does anyone else you know have my tracking power?" she asked Cailean.

"We have a diviner at the settlement who finds water whenever a well is needed." He sounded grumpy now, like the old druid. "Alick is a good boy who cares for his widowed mother. His family has served this clan for five generations. He wouldnae abduct Lamont's daughter."

"I never said he did," Diana said. They came to the edge of a blackberry thicket, and in the middle of it she saw a small, dingy-looking cottage. The amber trail took an abrupt turn and followed the narrow dirt path straight to the forester's front door. "Yep. He's got her."

Cailean glowered at her. "You cannae see that from here, Lieutenant."

"Call it a very solid, sparkly hunch." She walked the path through the brambles to the cottage, and heard a commotion inside. "Raen, keep your blades in their holsters, and let me do the talking." When he nodded she knocked on the door.

It opened, and a good-looking teenage boy with a pale, perspiring face stepped out and closed it behind him.

"Fair day to you, my lords, my lady," he said and gulped a little air. "We have sickness in the house, so I cannae invite you in. Do you, ah, wish to buy some firewood?"

Cailean heaved a sigh. "Alick, lad, what have you done?"

"Actually, Alick, lad," Diana said, "we've come for Lamont's daughter." A high-pitched shriek came from inside the cottage. "She's going to bolt," Diana told Raen. "You two should go around back now."

"I dinnae ken anything about N– Lady Nathara," Alick protested, and when Diana reached for the door he seized her hand. "Please, good, kind mistress. You mustnae do this."

"Sorry, kid. Not that kind."

She extricated her fingers before she pushed past him and went inside. The interior of the cottage looked much cleaner than the outside, although it was obvious the forester and his mother were poor. Beside a small fire in the hearth an old woman sat sewing on a beautifully embroidered piece of blue silk.

"Are you the mother?" Diana asked her.

"Aye," Alick's mother said. "Herself and the other one ran out the back." She jerked her head toward the rear of the cottage. "Has the maid dressed in her gown, the wee schemer."

The boy stepped in front of Diana. "Please, my lady."

"I'm sorry," she said and patted him on the shoulder. "Let's just try to end this before anyone gets hurt."

When she walked out the back of the cottage Diana found Raen and Cailean marching two red-faced, badly-scratched girls out of the thicket. The one dressed as the earl's daughter hung limp and wailed piteously, but the other fought and screeched every step of the way.

"Let go of me," Nathara demanded, the maid's cap slipping down over her face. "I have naught to do with this. I am a maid, I tell you."

"Sure," Diana said. "And I'm a monkey's uncle."

She watched as Alick rushed out and tried to take Nathara from Raen, who easily held him off with one hand. That made the earl's daughter scream and reach for him. Finally Diana put her fingers in her mouth and let out a loud, sharp whistle, silencing the three youngsters.

"Thank you," she said. "Now, let's go have a little chat."

Once back inside the cottage, all three teenagers tried to speak at once, while the forester's mother snorted and shook her head.

"Hey," Diana began. "*Hey.* If you don't shut up, I'm going to gag all of you." That quieted them down enough for her to talk at a normal level. "Thanks. Alick, start talking."

"I've ken Nathara since we were bairns, and my mother sewed for hers," the forester said. "I wouldnae harm her. I love her."

"And I him," the earl's daughter said,

sounding sulky. "I want nothing but to be his wife."

"More like she wanted to get away from the earl," the old lady put in. "She's the image of her mam, you ken. As long as he lives, he'll never let her marry. She'll go to her shroud an old maid."

"Speaking of which," Diana said and eyed the maid. "How did you get involved in this mess?"

"I didnae wish to take milady's jewels and bring them to the woodsman," the young maid said, sobbing the words. "She told me if I didnae she would tell her father I stole them."

"She did that anyway after you left," Diana assured her before she turned to Nathara. "You said good-bye to your father, went up to your room, and took off your gown. I'm guessing it was too big to let you fit in the basket."

"Aye, but I hated that gown," the girl said, lifting her chin. "'Twas my mother's and made for her. I wore it only to please my sire. 'Twas too plain and matronly for me."

"But you couldnae let your father find it," Raen said. "Else he might realize how you got out of the stronghold. That 'twas why you hid it behind your trunk."

"And then you climbed in the basket, covered

yourself with the mending, and let the servants carry you out," Cailean put in. "All Alick had to do was load the basket of mending onto his cart before he left."

Nathara uttered a petulant sound. "Why do you meddle in my affairs? I dinnae wish to return to my sire's household. I am a woman grown."

"We meddle, honey, because your dad thinks that the undead abducted you." Diana pointed at the maid. "And that you're a thief who stole his daughter's jewelry." She turned to Alick. "But he has no idea you helped smuggle your girl out of the stronghold. I wonder how he'll feel about that when I tell him. The guy has a lot of heavily-armed men working for him."

The boy went white. "Please, my lady, dinnae betray us."

Diana felt a pang of sympathy, and thought for a moment. "If we handle this the right way, we might be able to keep him from strangling the two of you before he locks up his daughter forever. Unless you want to die, or die a virgin, respectively." She glanced at Alick's mother. "She's still a virgin, right?"

"Naught of that until they were proper married, I told Alick. Made the wee schemer sleep with me last night to be sure." The old lady glanced at the maid. "And I told her she couldnae murder that one, no' after all the wench did to help them. 'Twouldnae be fair."

The maid let out a high-pitched shriek, and sagged against Cailean.

Nathara stamped her foot. "Now look what you've done," she snapped. "'Tis none of your concern, druidess." She gave Alick a pouty look. "And you. You said you would kill anyone who tried to take me from you."

"I was being manly," the boy protested. "You ken I've no weapons but my father's ax."

"Give it to me," his mother suggested, "and I'll fix this with one stroke." When she saw the look Raen gave her she smiled. "'Tis the simplest way. The maid can stay with me and Alick. Even if she hasnae a spine, I like her. She's a loyal little wench, and she cleans."

Diana glanced at Raen, who was pointedly staring at the ceiling beams. Cailean flapped his sleeve over the unconscious maid, trying to revive her. Nathara was examining the bleeding scratches from the brambles on her hands with a look of disgust. Alick had unmanly tears in his eyes.

Diana went over to check the maid, who aside from the scratches was fine.

"She's okay. She just fainted."

Alick sniffed loudly and swiped at his nose. With a little smile, Diana went to him and patted him on the back.

"Sometimes love is worth anything, kid," she said.

But as she said it, she realized how she could give everyone what they wanted *and* keep Lamont from discovering that his beloved daughter had tried to elope with her penniless beau.

"Okay, people," she said, clapping her hands. "New plan. Alick, get the ax."

Chapter Thirteen

✦✦✦

LATE THAT AFTERNOON Raen and Diana slipped away from the celebration at Lamont's stronghold and took the stream back to Skye. As they emerged from the spring pond at the edge of the glen, he saw Diana look around.

"Why did we come out here?" she asked. "The castle's miles away."

"I wished some time alone with you." He held onto her hand. "I reckon you needed the walk, too. Unless you'd rather run?"

"Walking's good," she said and climbed up the rocky slope to the path the villagers used to fetch water from the spring. "Do you think the earl will really let Alick marry Nathara?"

Raen grinned. "He was so grateful to have his

daughter returned to him I think *he* wished to wed Alick." He glanced at her. "Telling him that the forester rescued Nathara from the undead before we could was very smart. So was smearing the edge of the ax with the blood from Nathara's hands."

"You were the one who persuaded Lamont to grant Alick any reward he desired for his bravery," Diana countered. "I'm just glad that kid had the nerve to ask for Nathara's hand in marriage. The maid was overjoyed to stay and look after his mom, so everyone will live happily ever after, as it should be. You did good, Big Man."

A blurry image of Bradana came into his thoughts. His mortal wife would have died eventually, but he'd expected to have a long and happy marriage with her.

"No' everyone lives happily ever after, lass."

She tucked her arm through his. "You want to tell me about her, your wife?"

Raen usually hated even thinking about her, but suddenly the words spilled out of him.

"Her name was Bradana, and her people were orcharders on the mainland. The first time I saw her, I knew she was no' for me, but when she smiled it was as if the sunlight grew brighter, and the air warmer. I watched her from afar for a long time, wishing I could but hear her voice. Then I had to go closer, so I could hear it." He smiled, remembering. "She had a wonderful voice, like soft little bells ringing."

As they walked he described his slow and often painful courtship of his mortal love, and how he had tried to compromise between his love for Bradana and his duty to the clan.

"I couldnae run away with her, and she couldnae come to Dun Aran. It seemed we would forever be parted, and then one night, in a beautiful meadow where she picked wild flowers, she gave herself to me." He expected to feel the bitter resentment that came with those few, happy memories, but only a dull, sad ache entered his heart. "I couldnae keep taking from her and giving naught back."

"So you married her," Diana said, giving his arm a little squeeze.

"Aye. The very next day I brought her to a church, in a town far from her croft, and there we were wed. We still couldnae live together, but I saw her as often as I could." Raen endured a wave of shame before he said, "'Twas our deception that was our undoing. She should have told her family, but she lied to them, as I did to the laird and the clan."

"Someone found out?" Diana asked.

Raen nodded. "I used the pond in her croft when I went to see her. She would meet me there, and we would make love under the apple trees. One night a man who wanted to marry Bradana followed her, and saw me coming out of the pond. It takes a moment for my body to change, so he saw me as I am when I bond with the water. Then he watched me change back."

She made a low, hurt sound. "Oh, no."

"He told her people what he thought he saw," Raen said as he looked out at the horizon, where the sea and the sky seemed to mirror each other. "They were simple, superstitious folk, and assumed that she was consorting with a kelpie, that I was an evil water spirit, and Bradana a witch. The next day they tied her hands and feet, and put her to a witch test. If she didnae sink in the pond, she would be judged a witch. But when they pushed her in the water, it soaked her clothes and dragged her down beneath the water lilies. I found her body the next night, still tangled in them." Suddenly his throat was tight but he couldn't stop now. "She fought to free herself, you see. I think she fought until the moment she drowned."

Diana didn't say anything, but she pressed up against him, and stayed with him like that until he found his voice again.

"I carried her to the meadow she loved, where we had been happy, and I buried her there." Raen closed his eyes for a moment. "Then I went back, and made them tell me what they had done, and bring to me the man responsible. I put him in the pond, again and again, so he could ken her terror. As I did a storm came, and lightning struck the cottages and the orchards. That stopped me from drowning him, but half the croft burned to the ground that night."

"Raen," Diana whispered. Her arm came around him, and she cupped the back of his neck with her slim hand, rubbing it with a soothing motion. "I'm so sorry."

"Aye. 'Tis a sorry story." He held onto her for a long moment, and then released her. "Come. I need to walk now."

As they made their way across the glen, Raen pointed out some of the land Lachlan had given the villagers for new gardens, and the new fences the clan had erected to discourage the island's herds of wild red deer from raiding the crops. Diana stopped to admire the ancient stone bridge that arched over a melt water stream, and he refrained from telling her that he'd helped build it five hundred years in the past.

He wanted to tell her everything and decided to brace the laird about it as soon as Lachlan and Kinley returned from the mainland. Diana had proven time and again she could be trusted, and he was weary of withholding the full truth of what he was from her.

As they entered the sacred oak grove, she stopped and glanced around. "Hey, I know this place."

"'Tis where you crossed over, lass." He pointed at a wide circle formed of roots in the very center. "Just there."

Rather than move closer, Diana took a step back. "That's the spot." Her expression sobered as she dragged her teeth over her lower lip. "Druid Boy told me that I can go back through there to my time. Is that true?"

Something in her voice told Raen she didn't want that.

"I am not a druid, but Cailean doesnae lie about such things. We already ken you have the power to use the grove on your own. If you wished to, you might try now." Though he looked at her, she stared at the grove. "Diana?"

"Sorry. I spaced out a little there." She turned to face him. "I don't want to go back yet. Truth is, I may never want to." She ducked her head and ran her fingers along an edge of his tartan. "How would you feel if I stayed here? You being one of the reasons I would stay."

Raen gathered her in his arms, and tipped up her chin as he told her the truth. "Glad." He kissed her brow. "So glad." He touched his lips to the curve of her cheekbone. "Very, very glad," he murmured against her lips.

Diana's fingernails curled against his chest as she parted her lips for him, and moaned into his mouth. Raen took his time, giving her his tongue and tempting hers into his mouth. She tasted faintly of the celebratory whiskey Lamont had insisted they drink with him, and her own sweetness, which was far more intoxicating.

"I would have you again," he murmured against her lips. "'Tis all I can think anymore when I look upon you. I see you naked, under me, on me, and 'twould be so good. I grow hard every time I think of being inside you."

"And I go wet when I imagine you in me." She pressed herself against him, her long body trembling. "So I stay, and we do something about it."

"We could slip away tonight," he suggested, caressing her bottom. "The laird has a lodge in the ridges. 'Tis very private, and there is a bed."

"Make love in the laird's bed?" She looked wide-eyed at him. "You could get in trouble for that."

"We willnae tell him," Raen assured her, and kissed her again.

Dimly he heard someone clear their throat, and lifted his head to see Cailean standing on the other side of the circle.

The druid held up his long, pale hands. "I didnae mean to intrude, but I must speak with you. Diana, might I have a word with the seneschal alone?"

"Sure," she said, her face guarded. She stepped back from Raen. "I'll keep walking. Catch up when you can." Turning her head so Cailean couldn't see, she wiggled her eyebrows at him. "Think lodge."

He hated watching her go, and as soon as she was out of earshot he scowled at the druid.

"You saw for yourself how good and fair she

was today. She saved that lad's life, and placated Lamont, all without violence. She is druid kind, and yet you still treat her as if she were one of the undead."

"As it happens, Master Aber, I like the lieutenant very much," Cailean told him. "She is everything you say, and I think more than that. But before I came here, I went to the settlement to see my master. He convinced the conclave to send Diana back to her time."

A dull fury rose into Raen's head. "No. She doesnae wish to go. She just said thus to me. With her talent she could help us so much."

The druid made a calming gesture. "Bhaltair is determined to be rid of her, or he wouldnae have persuaded the others to rule so. There is more you should ken. Your laird openly disagreed with the ruling. He told the conclave that he would think on it, but it was clear to all that he willnae force her to go."

That news gave Raen some relief. "Then 'tis decided. Lachlan's word is law here."

"At the stronghold, aye." Cailean fell silent as he looked at the sacred circle. "Master Aber, the McDonnels have never flouted the conclave once in my memory. By doing so over this female, the laird challenges more than a ruling, do you understand that?"

He nodded slowly. "There will be trouble between us now."

"My master is a kind man, and a very wise one," the druid said. "He has accepted that the lieutenant didnae intend to harm him. 'Tis something else about her. In all of my incarnations, I have never seen him like this."

Raen thought of how Bhaltair had stared at Diana just before the gun fired, as if he couldnae believe his eyes. At the time he had assumed that her modern garments had astonished him, but now he was not so sure.

"Can you persuade him to change his thinking?" Raen asked.

"I will try, if I can." Cailean's expression grew bleak. "Bhaltair has great influence over our people, Master Aber. If the lieutenant doesnae return to her time, I fear he may take matters into his own hands. If it comes to that, 'twill cause a rift between the druids and the clan."

Chapter Fourteen

DIANA HAD ALMOST reached the path through the ridge to the stronghold when Raen and Cailean finally caught up with her.

"There you are," she said. "I thought you might have gone back to Lamont's for another drink."

"The clan is likely still celebrating," Cailean said. "You did very good work there, Lieutenant."

While the druid went on praising her ingenuity in peacefully reuniting the earl with his daughter, the big man remained silent. Diana guessed their private chat had been about her, or whatever the laird didn't want Raen to tell her. As impatient as she felt over being left out, she couldn't fault the big man for keeping secrets. She

was still hanging on to a rather large one of
her own.

When they reached the stronghold, Cailean
went directly to the dovecote to check for any
messages, while Raen spoke to the sentries before
escorting Diana to his rooms in the upper hall.
Once inside he took a bottle from a cabinet,
uncorked it, and poured some very dark liquid
into two goblets.

"So we're still partying," she said drily as she
accepted the cup and sat down to watch him pace
around her. "Or is this a bon voyage drink?" His
blank expression forced her to add, "Are the
druids sending me home? You can tell me. I won't
say anything."

"The conclave has ruled that you must return
to your time," he said. He drained his goblet and
refilled it. "'Twas Bhaltair's doing, Cailean said."
He met her gaze. "The laird told them he would
think on it. 'Tis Lachlan's way of refusing
politely."

"You know, I really like your laird." She took a
swallow from her cup, and the contents burned a
hot, sweet path down her throat. "What is
this stuff?"

"Bran'y, I think. Evander left it." He turned

the bottle in his hand. "I dinnae want you to leave."

"But there will be problems if I stay," she predicted.

"Aye." He put the bottle and goblet on the mantle and sat down on the floor in front of her to stare into the flames. "I cannae understand it. They didnae demand this of Kinley."

"That's because she was brought here by the sacred grove. I just tripped and fell into your time." Diana saw how tense his shoulders were, and began rubbing them. "I don't want to cause trouble between the clan and the holy folks. If there's no other way, I'll go back. I'll want some major lodge time with you first, but I will."

"No," he said simply. He caught her hands and held them as he looked up at her. "Promise me you willnae go."

"It's not up to me, but I'll try." Her heart felt like it was knotting and dissolving, all at once. "Maybe if we give them a good reason to keep me around, that will help. I was able to track down Lamont's daughter easy enough. You don't have cops here. When people go missing, what do you do?"

"We search, but when we find them they're

almost always…" He went still and his eyes shifted left and right before he looked up at her. "Diana, I ken how you can stay."

Before she could answer the door opened and Neac peered in at them. "The laird and lady have returned, and they're asking for you both."

Diana went down to the great hall with Raen and the chieftain, where Lachlan and Kinley were being fussed over by Meg.

"I've plenty more in the kitchen," the chatelaine told the men as she set out soup and bread for the pair. "Yer new gown is very fetching, milady. Will ye not wear it now and again, so we might recall ye're a lass?"

Kinley, who looked like a goddess in her golden and blue velvet gown, grinned at the old woman.

"If it makes you happy, Meg, I'll put it on every Sunday." Her gaze shifted. "There you are, Lieutenant. Cailean was just telling us that you found an earl's missing daughter *and* arranged her marriage, all in one day."

"It's still the job, Captain," Diana told her, and smiled at Raen. "I had plenty of help from your cop." She nodded to the laird. "Lamont says hey, and thanks."

"We are in your debt, Diana." Lachlan rose and bowed to her. "I fear we dinnae return with happy news. The conclave didnae rule in your favor."

Neac glared at Cailean. "We might beat some sense into the magic folk. They'll no' put up much of a fight."

"How often can they be rebirthed?" Tormod asked. "They've been doing it for so long now they might have worn out the magic womb."

Cailean gave the Norseman a narrow look. "Our magic doesnae wear out, Master Liefson. Would you like me to prove it?"

"There will be no beatings or shows of magic," Raen said flatly before he regarded the laird. "The lieutenant is the best tracker I have ever seen, my lord. With only a few clues she worked out how the lass got away, and then took us directly to her. 'Tis a talent sorely needed by the clan, especially now."

That startled Diana. "Why, did someone else go missing?"

"Aye, our enemies," the laird said. "It shames me that you would so generously serve the clan's ally, when we have done naught but treat you as a prisoner." He looked around at his men. "That ends now."

"So you'll treat me like clan?" The moment Diana asked that a lightbulb went off in her brain. "Or could you make me a member of the clan?"

Kinley uttered a cry of delight. "That's it." She turned to her husband. "If Diana is a McDonnel, then the druids have no say over what happens with her. Only you do. She'll be like me. We can even form our own search and rescue team." She turned to Cailean. "Am I right?"

The druid looked askance at Diana. "She is druid kind. Being made clan willnae change that. We dinnae have say over you, my lady, because you are the laird's wife."

"So the lass could wed a McDonnel, and become clan by marriage," Neac said, and glared at Raen. "A bonnie prospect for any man."

"Before anyone announces my engagement," Diana said quickly, "why don't we let the laird talk?"

"Thank you, Lieutenant," Lachlan said dryly. "Becoming a member of the clan is no' simply taking our name as protection. You would be subject to my rule, and treated as any other

McDonnel. We would use you as our tracker when we hunt the undead."

"My lord, I think 'tis no' wise to cross Master Flen," Cailean put in.

The laird ignored him. "'Tis much you yet dinnae ken about us, Diana, but once you are made clan, 'twill be revealed to you. You cannae change your mind on this once you are a McDonnel, so be sure."

"Well, you don't know everything about me, either," Diana said but eyed Kinley. "Did it change your mind?" When the captain shook her head, she turned to Raen. "Any second thoughts about having me stay?"

Raen brought his hands up to her face, and kissed her, slowly and deliberately, before he lifted his head and smiled. "I think of naught else, my lady."

Neac beamed, Tormod groaned, and Kinley applauded.

"My lord, you should be aware that Diana bears my mark." Raen lifted her palm to show the jag of ink to the laird. "So I and my spirit would very much like her to stay."

"You have been busy, Seneschal," Lachlan

said. He stood and shouted, "Clan McDonnel, attend me."

Every clansman within earshot came rushing into the hall, and gathered around them until they were completely surrounded by grim-faced highlanders. Diana moved closer to Raen, who folded his hand over hers.

"'Tis good to be home, brothers," Lachlan said. "While my lady and I were away, Raen Aber, Cailean Lusk, and our guest, Lieutenant Burke, searched for and found Lamont's only child. Since the earl is an important ally, 'twas a boon to this clan. 'Twas the lieutenant's druid talent that led our men to the lass. She has a powerful gift for tracking that which doesnae wish to be found."

Murmurs swept through the hall.

The laird lifted his hand, and the clansmen fell silent. "The druid conclave has ruled to send the lieutenant back to her homeland. I believe them wrong. I believe the sacred grove brought her to us, as it brought my wife. I believe Diana Burke was sent by the Gods to join our clan and aid in our quest. If any of you wouldnae have her as our sister, tell me now."

No one made a sound, but most of the highlanders looked at Diana as if they had never before seen her. Then someone shouted in a strange language, and the men made way for the stable master, who came stumbling forward with a bottle in his hand.

"I dinnae want her," Seoc said, and swayed on his feet as he peered at Diana. "The last mortal wench kept prisoner here took my cousin from me. She lured him away with her wiles." He stabbed a finger at Lachlan. "And you did naught about it."

"Aye, 'tis true," Lachlan said. "But Evander and Fiona are gone now, and I've no' the heart to pursue them." The laird put a hand on the stable master's shoulder. "Diana is no' a legion spy. She is a warrior like Kinley, and she has proven her worth. I cannae deny her because she has done nothing to betray the clan."

Seoc stiffened. "While Evander did for his whore. Aye, I ken that, my lord. I live with it every day, crushing me." He gave Diana a bleary grin. "And now this one to see, to remind me of my shame. Perhaps she should. I take back my objection." He turned around and staggered out of the hall.

"Any others wish to speak against it?" the laird said mildly.

No one said a word.

"If she's clan I'll not have to chase her every morning," Tormod said loudly, and scowled at Diana. "Aye, join us, Red. My legs want the rest."

Some of the men chuckled, but a good many pushed forward, and one said, "We Uthars would hear what our chieftain thinks."

"She may be a mortal, and a wench, but she fights like a man, runs like a deer, and drinks like an Uthar," Neac said. "Aye, I'll be proud to call her kin."

"Mortal?" Diana murmured to Raen. "Doesn't he mean druid kind?"

"Wait for it," he advised her gravely.

"Well, then," Lachlan said and drew a short dagger from his belt. He held it over his head. "We're for the loch, lads."

Diana walked with Raen as they followed the laird and the clan out of the castle and down to the edge of the water. Storm clouds shadowed the setting sun, and distant lightning flashed, illuminating the horizon like bombs detonating. When she glanced at the big man she saw his ink wasn't lighting up or moving, but he looked a little grim.

Lachlan stood by two tall, carved stones and

beckoned to Diana. Raen released her hand and said, "Go to him, and kneel before the stones."

Diana felt something crackling in the air as she made her way through the crowd of clansmen to the laird. He moved to stand between the stones, and she dropped down before him.

Lachlan took her hand, and wrapped it around the hilt of his blade. He folded his hand on top of hers, and Neac used a very old piece of cord to bind her wrist to the laird's.

As the chieftain spoke in another, unfamiliar language, Lachlan translated, and told Diana to repeat the words.

"I pledge myself to Lachlan McDonnel, laird of the McDonnel, as his clanswoman. From this day I am sister to him and his brothers," she said. "When called upon by the clan, I shall always answer. I shall fight their battles, protect their allies, and keep their secrets. This I swear on my soul and my life."

The clan let out a blood-curdling war cry, which made Diana jump a little. But as soon as the laird helped her to her feet and untied their hands he embraced her.

"I've never had brothers," she told him as she

drew back. "I've always been alone. You might have to give me lessons."

"We are your family now, lass," Lachlan said. "We will give you anything you need."

The men began diving into the loch, their bodies radiating power as they transformed, and soon the water glowed with sparkling light. Lachlan and Raen joined them, leaving Diana with Kinley.

"They're giving us a chance to talk," the laird's wife explained. "Lachlan thought I should be the one to tell you."

"They're like kids," Diana said, smiling as she saw a transparent Neac leap out of the water, change briefly, and splash back down. "Okay, what's the big secret?"

"About twelve hundred years ago the McDonnels were Pritani, also known as the Picts," Kinley told her. "They protected the druids from the Romans when they invaded. Their final battle with the Ninth Legion was here, on Skye. All of the tribesmen came to fight, but the Romans outnumbered them three to one. They lost and were captured."

Diana grimaced. "That must have sucked."

"What came after was worse." Her expression

grew bleak. "When the Pritani wouldn't tell the Romans where the druids were hiding, the legion slaughtered them, and threw their bodies into the loch. All of the Pritani tribesmen died that day, right here."

"God, that's horrible," Diana said, feeling sick. "But if the legion killed all of them, then how could the clan be descended from…" She stopped and stared at Kinley as she thought of Neac calling her a mortal. "Oh, no."

"The druids came here, and used their magic to bring the Pritani back from the dead," Kinley said softly. "When they did that, they cast their deaths onto the Ninth Legion, and turned the Romans into the undead. Lachlan and Raen and all of the McDonnels *are* the men who died here twelve hundred years ago. The clan was made immortal, Diana. They never have to die again."

Chapter Fifteen

❦

DIANA LEFT KINLEY by the loch and grabbed a torch before she headed for the glen. At first she walked blindly, finding her way down the ridge path by instinct. Once she stepped out of the rocks she stared at the wide, grassy plain, and how the moonlight made everything look ghostly. The panorama certainly went along with the big freaking castle, the resurrected highlanders, and their undead enemies. No dragons, though. She'd been half-hoping for some scaly, jewel-eyed beast to slither out of the dungeon to send her a telepathic *Heya*.

She hadn't just joined a clan of immortals. She'd fallen in love with one. One who along with all the others had been killed. Slaughtered. Right here.

Diana started jogging across the glen. The flame of her torch whipped wildly over her head, and she stumbled a few times, but she didn't fall or stop. Soon she was running, her legs taking the long, bouncing strides she'd used in college to win three state track competitions. She didn't have to stop. She could run until she couldn't think anymore, until she couldn't imagine what it had been like for Raen—

A wide stream flashed in front of her, too wide to jump. Diana tried to run through it, lost her footing and was swept off and hurled over a shelf of rocks into a deep pool of cold water.

She surfaced, sputtering as more water crashed down on her head. Submerging, she swam a few yards and resurfaced to see the water-fall she'd gone over. It looked almost as high as the cliff she'd thought Kinley had jumped off back in Horsethief Canyon. Her now-extinguished torch floated up to bob on the waves, and that was when she realized the pool of water and the rocks surrounding it were being lit by something else, something that was flashing over her head.

Diana looked up to see a huge storm cloud

spreading over her, its dark billowy mass crawling with lightning, and felt two big, strong arms reach around her. She hated how wonderful it felt, as if nothing mattered but being with him.

"If you were trying to sneak up on me, your spirit blew it."

"You knew I would follow," Raen said and turned her around to face him. The flashing overhead echoed in his gray eyes. "I am the same man I was, Diana. Naught has changed but what you ken of my past. But if 'tis too much, tell me now, and I will leave you be."

"Too much?"

She pushed him away, swam to the edge of the pool, and hoisted herself out. She would have run from there back to the castle, but her legs felt like gelatin, her head was spinning, and she couldn't catch her breath. It shocked her to realize she was furious with him.

Raen climbed out and started to reach for her, and then apparently thought better of it.

"You are angry, I understand. I had no choice. I couldnae tell you. 'Tis clan law. Only those pledged to us can be told."

"It's a huge secret. I get it." She braced her hands on her knees and gulped in air. "I don't care about that."

He moved a little closer. "Then why did you run?"

"It's a nice night," Diana said, and straightened to glare at him. "I've missed my morning jogs. Oh, and back at the castle? I was standing on the place where *you were murdered twelve hundred years ago.*"

Raen frowned. "You are shouting at me because the Romans killed me there? 'Twas not as if I chose the spot."

"Shut up," she said, just as her legs decided to give out. She dropped to the ground and propped her head against her hands. "God. You think knowing you're an immortal is too much for me? You *died*, Raen. You died a horrible death here on this island, and then you built a castle, and you live here, like it's nothing? When I think of what they must have…"

Her imagination generated all manner of grotesque images. She shook her head as though that might stop them.

Raen crouched down beside her. "You are wrong about this, lass. 'Twas quick for me. The laird had it much worse. They left him for last, to make him watch." He rubbed his knuckles down her cheek. "Fack me, I am sorry. Dinnae cry."

Diana turned her face away and swiped her fingers over her wet cheeks. "No wonder you treat the druids like all-powerful beings. Crap, they really are."

"The clan is grateful to them," Raen said as he stretched out his legs and leaned back on his elbows. "But I sometimes wonder if we should be."

Her jaw dropped. "Excuse me? You're not happy being immortal? You never have to die. That's the ultimate gift. In fact, *nothing* says thank you like eternal life."

"It seems a boon, until time begins to pass, and naught changes for you," Raen told her. "We cannae live as we did, as men who take wives, and have families, and pass our skills onto the next born. No bairns have been born to any of us since the awakening. We dinnae age, while all the mortals around us do. Even our creation had a terrible price. When the magic folk brought us back, they used the same spell to curse the Romans, and that created the undead."

"Is that why they didn't reverse the spell? Because the clan would have to die again?" She nodded, answering her own question. "Cailean told me that big magic has big consequences."

"Aye," Raen said. He reached over and took her marked hand, turning it over to trace the transferred ink. "But it brought us together, and that I cannae regret."

She sighed, but then a thought occurred to her. She gave him a sideways glance.

"Does my joining the clan make us like actual brother and sister?"

Raen laughed. "You are my sister in arms, no' my blood kin. For that you would have to be born Pritani, and our tribes have been gone for centuries." His expression sobered. "I am sorry that Seoc Talorc spoke as he did. That was more about his cousin than you, lass."

"He's hurting, and drinking, which is never a great combination." Diana lay down beside him to look up at the storm cloud, which seemed to be dispersing. "I won't be locked up in the tower anymore, which will be nice. Where am I going to live now?"

"The laird will give you rooms," Raen said and turned on his side. With one fingertip he traced the sweep of her brow before he said, "Or you could share mine."

Diana suppressed a little grin and gave him a solemn look.

"I don't know if that's such a good idea. There's not enough space for me to do my yoga. Also, it's super dreary, and you only sleep there."

"I will burn all of Evander's things, which will make room for you and your yoga and your grain sacks." Raen ran his finger down her nose, over her lips and chin and kept going to her navel. "The bed I must keep, as 'tis one of the few large enough for us to share."

"Really." She glanced down to see him tugging her shirt from her trousers, and had to smile. "So we're sharing a bed, too."

"We willnae always sleep in it." He slid his big hand under her shirt and rubbed his palm over her belly. "I will show you how 'twill be tonight, if you wish."

Diana curled an arm around his neck. "Maybe you should show me now."

Raen's dark, shaggy hair fell to curtain her face as he kissed her, his mouth teasing hers until she caught his lower lip between her teeth and ran her tongue across it. He buried his hands in her hair as he deepened the kiss, his mouth demanding more, and Diana groaned as the heat and hunger billowed inside her.

By the time he ended the passionate embrace he was on his back, with her on top of him, and she sat up to strip off her shirt. He reached for her bra, gently feeling the pattern of the black lace until he found the front fastener.

"Like this," she said, opening it for him. She leaned back as he peeled away the cups to slowly fondle her. The way he stroked her nipples made her rub her crotch over the thick bulge straining the front of his trousers. "By the way, I don't wear a bra in bed."

"Shameless wench," he chided as he drew the straps down her arms. "You should wear it always. I like it. 'Tis lovely, and a little wicked—like you."

That inspired her. "Then you're really going to like this."

Raen watched as she moved back to sit on his thighs, and then jerked as she unfastened his trousers and released the hard, swollen length of his shaft. He smiled as she wrapped her fingers around him, but when she bent her head he took in a sharp breath.

"Lass, you dinnae have to do this for…ah." His head fell back as she put her mouth over the broad bulb of his cockhead and stroked it with her tongue. "'Tis so good."

Diana went to work, taking as much of his penis into her mouth as she could with each glide of her lips. He was so long and wide she could manage only a little over half before she ran out of room, but she compromised by curving her hands around and stroking the rest of him as she sucked and licked.

Raen braced himself on his elbows, his eyes dark slits now as he watched her love him with her mouth. When she met his gaze she let him slide almost all the way out, and then tugged on him as she flicked her tongue around the flared ridge of his glans. He shuddered deeply, his thighs knotting under her and his chest heaving.

Now that she had his full attention, Diana leaned in, cradling his lower shaft between the curves of her breasts and pressing them in with her arms so her mounds massaged him. She played with his cockhead, kissing and licking it while she moved up and down, sliding his length through her cleavage.

She took her mouth away but kept him pinned between her breasts. "Still want me to wear a bra to bed?"

"Naked," he said, his voice dropping so low it rumbled. "I want you naked, in my bed, everywhere, all the time. Only I will have to beat into the ground anyone who looks at you. Be naked only for me, lass, and I willnae ever get out of my bed."

"Okay," Diana said and grinned. "But that means you have to sleep bare-assed, too."

"If you insist," he said, and groaned as she once more engulfed him with her lips.

She slowly sucked and stroked him until she felt sure he was about to come, and then reached down to tenderly caress his tight balls with her fingers. As she held him in her mouth, she did the same to his shaft with her tongue. Feeling the first surge of his come jolt through his shaft excited her as much as the groans of pleasure that spilled from his throat. So did seeing the ink on his face pulse with light.

Raen drew her up and held her against his hard chest. "You are bold, lass."

"Well, you are delicious, lad." The feel of his hands stroking her back made her wriggle with delight, and then she felt the hardness of his new erection against her belly. "And very enthusiastic. Stay right there and hold that thought."

Diana rolled away to strip off the rest of her clothes, a task Raen finished for her before he pulled her on top of him.

"When you are naked, I cannae wait." He lifted her by the hips, positioning her over his erect cock before lowering her to be impaled. "Oh, Diana."

"This is your fault." She propped her hands on his shoulders as she sank down on him, the soaked folds of her pussy flowering around the iron-hard column of his penis. The slow, deep penetration felt so perfect that she didn't want it to end. "Keep this up and we're never going to sleep again."

When she had taken him all the way down to his throbbing root, Diana bent over to kiss him, and pressed her marked hand against his ink. The spirit's power poured into her, racing through her palm, up her arm and into her chest. It sent twin surges of tingling heat up her neck and down into her breasts. She felt her nipples grow engorged as she rose again and drew his hands to cover them, biting her lip as he rubbed and squeezed her.

The air around them began to snap with tiny white sparks that pinged off her skin to fall and disappear into his chest.

Diana laughed out loud, feeling as if she were dancing in a shower of light as she rode his beautiful cock. Enveloping and caressing his shaft with her softness made nothing else matter but him, as need and pleasure clashed inside her belly. She tried to keep it at bay by slowing and clenching around him, but that let her feel every inch of his thick, heavy shaft. She lost herself to the joy of taking it inside, deeper and harder and faster.

Raen dragged her down to his chest, kissing her as he clamped his hands on her bottom. From that moment he took over, thrusting into her like a frenzied piston, his cock plowing so deep Diana lost all control, her hands bunching in his hair and her cries spilling into his mouth.

The storm crashed over Diana, but it came from within, from his relentless fucking, and made her come with it. She gripped him inside and flooded him with the cascade of her release, dragging him in with her. She felt him groaning and shaking under her, made helpless by the tight hold of her clenching, pulsating sex. He was hers.

The air grew colder as they lay locked together, and the last spasms of their orgasm finally faded. Their panted breaths drifted away in opaque white puffs. He held a hand on her bottom, gently caressing it while he stayed half-erect inside her. Diana idly stroked his chest as she listened to his powerful heart, and imagined waking up every morning for the rest of her life, hearing it. She wouldn't live as long, but whatever time they had would be wonderful.

"Dinnae worry," he murmured, and when she lifted her head he added, "I can feel your frown on my flesh. Tell me what troubles you. We have no more secrets to keep."

Panic flashed through her, as she still had one extremely large, extra-hideous secret. She couldn't tell him now, when they'd just loved each other senseless. Since she could stay, it really didn't matter anymore.

"I was just wondering what I'd do if you kick me out of your bed." She kissed his chin. "I don't think you'll be able to, pal. You're stuck with me. You might even be stuck *in* me."

"A man can dream." His expression softened as he cradled her cheek. "But I dinnae have to anymore. You are my dream."

"That's good," she said, and hugged him tightly. "Because you're mine."

Chapter Sixteen

❧❧❧

FROM THE BATTLEMENTS of Ermindale Castle, Quintus looked out at the dark territory that now belonged to the Ninth Legion. From where he stood he could see the ocean's faint glimmer to the north, and breathed in the fresh tang of the salt-laced air. An elderly miser with a fading reputation for ruthlessness, the Marquess of Ermindale had put up only a token resistance when Quintus had arrived with his occupation force. As soon as the castle's few guards were overwhelmed, the nobleman had scurried off with his family and personal retainers to the solar, where they had barricaded themselves inside. Quintus had ordered the scanty remainder of the staff enthralled, and left the marquess and his kin to stew.

The new enthrallment he had used on the earl
and his doomed countess at their castle made the
conquest of this stronghold so much more
satisfying.

Everything Quintus had worked for over the
last year now lay within reach. In another month
the thousands of men still in hiding would arrive
at Ermindale. By then the new stronghold had to
be ready for occupation, and a steady source of
blood thralls acquired to feed the men. The latter
was his most pressing dilemma. All of the men
were slowly starving, and because of it would
descend into madness the moment they smelled
fresh mortal blood. In that state they would hunt
in packs like mindless beasts, and kill until the
sun's deadly rays burned them to ash.

He was so close. He could not allow the legion
to be destroyed by their curse.

"Tribune Seneca," Brutus Ficini said. The
veteran centurion joined him and slapped his
forearm across his chest. "How may I serve?"

"Our scouts have reported finding a settlement hidden in the hills to the east," Quintus said
as he removed his red battle cloak. "I will require
a raiding party of fifty, on horseback, within the
hour." He draped the paludamentum over Ficini's

broad shoulders. "I shall accompany the party, but you will lead them."

Ficini looked uneasy. "A centurion of the Ninth is not permitted to wear the red into battle, sir."

"Then it is good that I am promoting you to the rank of *praefectus*." He clipped his cloak to the older man's armor and smiled a little. "You are my second now, Brutus. I wish your counsel on all matters important to the legion."

"I am grateful for the promotion, Tribune," his new prefect told him. "I wish only to advise you that a settlement raid will be dangerous now. The men have been on lean rations for some weeks. As they are now, when blood is spilled, they will go into a frenzy. I suggest those chosen for the party first be fed."

"Agreed. Give them the last of the blood thralls we brought with us." Quintus checked the position of the moon. "I must go down and check on the progress with the tunnels. I will meet you and the men at the stables in one hour."

Ficini saluted him again, turned smartly, and walked along the curtain wall to the entry to the garrison.

Quintus took the tower stairs to the castle's

cellars, where several dozen men worked to exca-
vate the new tunnels. Seeing their progress
pleased him, for they had dug out three passages
that smelled of sea water. When the centurions
supervising the work came to report to him, he
learned the men were half the way to the sea
caves by the marquess's docks.

"I can send a team to dig from the other
direction, Tribune," the overseer told him as he
spread out the scroll with the excavation plans on
a work table. "But if we do not shore up the shafts
as we go along here, and here, there is great risk
of collapse. We are so close to the surface now
that I fear the ground would sink. Should that
happen, we would be forced to abandon the
tunnel and start over at a more distant point."

"Continue as you do now," he told the men.
"Avoid anything that will expose the passages."

Quintus retrieved his weapons from the
marquess's study, which he had taken over as his
command center, and issued close-guard orders to
his sentry commander before he went out to the
stables. The men had already saddled and
mounted their horses. Ficini led out his favorite
mare and handed the reins to him.

"I spoke with the scouts, Tribune," his prefect said as he stepped back. "They advise we follow the crooked river east for three leagues, and go in by water, not land. There is some manner of barrier around the place."

Druids often concealed their settlements, and Quintus had yet to test the new enthrallment on them. If he could enslave the heathens, they might know how to force the McDonnels to remove the undead curse.

"Lead us there, Prefect Ficini."

From Ermindale the raiding party rode along the river until they reached woods too thick and overgrown to be passable. There they guided their mounts into the rushing water, which proved shallow, and continued until their front riders signaled a stop.

The full moon had reached its apex in the night sky, and bathed the small settlement in pale light. There were two dozen thatched cottages surrounding a cluster of oaks. White-berried mistletoe vines draped the tree branches so heavily they appeared as if covered by snow.

Ficini dismounted, and signaled his men to do the same. Once they tethered their horses on the riverbank he assembled the ranks into a raid formation. Then he marched them to the edge of the settlement.

"Parati," he said, keeping his voice low, and the men drew their swords and held them ready. *"Impetus."*

Quintus watched from his mare as the raiding party poured into the settlement and began dragging mortals out of the cottages. He felt gratified when he saw they wore the robes of druids, and urged his mount forward as Ficini and his men herded the heathens into a tight cluster beneath the mistletoe.

Once the men had searched every cottage, and brought forth their occupants, Quintus dismounted and joined his prefect.

"Well done, Brutus," the tribune said and surveyed the faces of their captives. "These should provide enough to keep the excavators fed for the next moon."

Ficini nodded, but looked puzzled. "Why do they not resist, Tribune?"

"We dinnae fear you, Roman." An elderly man moved to the front of the group and regarded Quintus. "Indeed, we foresaw your coming."

"And yet you remained to greet us," he said, smiling a little. "You cannot terrify me with your claims of magic, old man. We know your kind. You have no true power, and waving your little twigs at us will not spare you." He looked at the calm faces of the druids around the elderly one. "If you wish to live, you must serve us."

The old druid produced a long, thin dagger. "Always we live." He turned the blade inward, and drove it into his heart. He toppled over at Quintus's boots as the other druids drew their blades.

Ficini shouted orders for the men to disarm the heathens, but by then it was done. Every mortal captive lay on the ground, dead by their own hands. The white berries from the mistletoe vines began to rain down on their bodies, first slowly and then like rain, until they nearly buried the corpses under a blanket of white.

"Don't touch them," Quintus said when one of the centurions reached for the body of a young, pretty woman. "The berries are poisonous, and have fallen onto their wounds. Their blood will be tainted now." He removed his helmet and dragged his hand through his damp hair. "Search the houses again."

The men turned up nothing but a few old, primitive sickles and baskets filled to the brim with the white, waxen berries.

"It seems odd that they have no children here," Ficini said as the last searchers returned. "And why would they grow and collect poisonous berries?"

"No doubt they use them in their heathen rituals," Quintus said. He mounted his mare and looked down on the mound of mistletoe that now completely covered the dead druids. What the old man had said gnawed at him, as if it had been more than a desperate taunt. "Leave them and return to the castle."

The ride back to Ermindale gave Quintus time to consider the mass suicide. The legion almost never captured druids. Just before Gaius Lucinius's fall they had taken a pair, but the two were later released by Fiona Marphee and her McDonnel lover. They had, in fact, gone to great lengths and endangered themselves to do so. The clan had always been fiercely protective of their heathen allies. As mortals they had gone to their deaths rather than betray them. Such was their loyalty that their gods had given them eternal life…

Always we live.

When Quintus arrived back at the castle, he ordered Ficini to accompany him to the highest level of the stronghold, where the marquess and his family remained locked in the family rooms. As soon as the legion had invaded the main house, they had retreated to the solar and blocked the door. A small opening had been broken through a row of latticework in the otherwise thick door. Quintus had considered lighting a fire by the door and directing the smoke through the hole to drive out the nobles, but other, more important matters had distracted him.

"How are we to pry that old man and his women out of these rooms?" Quintus murmured, half to himself.

"I can send for the battering ram, Tribune," the prefect suggested.

Quintus shook his head, and looked through the hole. On the other side the marquess sat before a cold hearth, his frail body wrapped in tartans. On impulse he called to the man.

"My Lord Ermindale, come here, that we may parlay."

The old man rose and hobbled over, ducking his head to peer with rheumy eyes at Quintus.

"You have my stronghold and my people, Roman. What more can you want from me and mine?"

"We raided a druid settlement tonight," he told the marquess. "I offered to spare their lives if they served us. They killed themselves, all of them. Why?"

Ermindale made a contemptuous sound. "Why should I tell you anything, Roman?"

"I can send for the battering ram," Quintus reminded him. "And my men are very hungry."

"They did themselves in because they are magic folk," the old man spat the words. "They cannae die a true death. They come back again and again."

Quintus had heard the old myth many times, and had scoffed at it. Now it gave him pause.

"You believe this?"

"I ken it, stupit, because I've seen it done. The druid that served my father died of old age when I first married. Twenty years later he returned to serve me. He looked a different man, but he remembered all of his former life. He spoke of things he couldnae ken. He revealed secrets my father had taken with him to his grave."

"He might have learned that from the elder druid before he died," Quintus pointed out.

"My father's druid played the pipes," the old man said. "It takes a lifetime to master. When he returned rebirthed as a young man, he could play any I asked, as well as the last." His eyes narrowed. "Why do you doubt it? Your kind never die. 'Twas the talk of the king's court when I last went."

Quintus suspected the marquess knew many things that would be useful, but he had to get the old man out of the solar before he could enthrall him.

"Your counsel is appreciated, Ermindale. Come out of there, and I give you my word that you will be well-treated."

"We'll be made slaves," the old man countered. "Used and drained and then tossed away like rotted whiskey casks. I'd rather starve than feed your kind." His eyes shifted left and he lowered his voice. "But give me what I want, and you will have my counsel. I can tell you how to get all the blood slaves you need. Indeed, I ken a way in which you may take control of Scotland."

Ficini made a rude sound, but Quintus felt

reluctantly intrigued. "What do you want, Ermindale?"

"To never die," the marquess said. "Make me one of you. Make me undead."

Chapter Seventeen

MIST ROLLED ACROSS the dark fields to float over the road from the village, and made Diana's face feel as cold and damp as the night air. It'd taken a couple of weeks, but she'd finally gotten used to riding Treun, the big, muscular gelding Raen had given her to use on patrol—aka the most patient horse in the fourteenth century—but she felt frustrated as she scanned the area.

"They didn't leave the road here," she told him. "They kept going."

"Then so shall we," he said, and raised his arm to gesture for the warband to continue riding forward.

They had been summoned from their search

for the undead to look for a tiny band of villagers who had disappeared earlier in the day. Diana hadn't found any signs of force or struggle in the fields where they had been working. The animals and tools they had been using had simply been left behind. She had tracked the people to this one road, but once they had reached it their individual trails converged with those of every other person who had used it. Just her luck, it happened to be a very busy road.

But at least she didn't see any of the dull red trails the legion left.

Although nine people simply didn't simultane- ously walk away from their lives, this wasn't the first missing group that had been reported. Over the past month dozens of mortals from towns, villages, and even well-guarded strongholds had done the same. The assumption had been that they were being abducted, until they'd discovered each time that the undead were responsible.

"Kinley told me that last year she and the laird had been trying to pinpoint the location of the undead lair by triangulating the reported attacks," Diana said to Raen. "Have you ever thought about doing the same thing with these mass disappearances?"

"The undead are never seen near them," he pointed out.

"But we know they're making zombies out of some of the people who go missing," she muttered to her lover as they went over a wide bridge. "I hate rescuing them when they're zombies. They never say thank you. They're too busy trying to stab us with farm implements."

"When we kill the undead who enthralled them, their control over them ends," he reminded her.

"Unless they turn themselves into human body shields," Diana said and shuddered, remembering one sweet-faced girl who during a battle had impaled herself on a clansman's sword in an attempt to keep him from killing her fanged master. "We need to stop it from happening."

He guided his mount closer to hers. "Once Cailean discovers exactly the manner they use to enthrall the mortals so completely, he will devise a potion that will break their dominion."

"The few we have brought back don't remember anything." Diana said and sighed. "Druid Boy needs help."

That was the other problem that nagged at her. Since the night she'd joined the clan the druids had been boycotting the McDonnels. None of the magic folk came to the island, spoke to the highlanders, or even sent messages by dove. She was also sure that the only reason Cailean still remained at Dun Aran was because Bhaltair had ordered him to keep her under surveillance.

A clansman rode up between them, startling Diana.

"Fair night to you, Sister," Seoc said, for once sounding sober. "Might I guard your flank?" He drew his sword and made a flashy, three-sixty swing with it. "'Twould ease my conscience."

She exchanged a look with Raen before she smiled at the stable master. "We've got this, Seoc, but thanks."

"Have a care with her, Seneschal. She is yet easy to kill." He wheeled around to return to his former position.

"It was nice of the laird to send him on patrol with us," Diana said. "He needs to feel like he's included."

Raen watched him and then shook his head. "Something is amiss with Seoc. He hasnae touched a dram of whiskey since we gave him Evander's things. I wonder if 'twas a mistake."

"It was," Diana replied. "Kinley said he tried to throw it all in the loch." Diana felt a little worried about the stable master, too. "She had to convince him to cart the stuff down to the village and let the locals have it."

Peering ahead to see the condition of the road, Diana reined in Treun and dismounted, prompting her lover to do the same. She dropped down to examine a deep, fresh gouge in the hard-packed surface of the road, but found only a horseshoe with two broken nails hanging askew.

"Four-legged, not two," she told Raen as she turned to toss the shoe off the road, and saw something else. "Wait, I've got some boot marks here leading into the field."

She had to wave away the mist as she peered at the multiple prints left in the soil. They over-lapped, but she was able to distinguish individual marks left by the soles, and counted nine distinct sets.

"This is them," she said. "They got off the road here."

Raen looked up at the hills rising to the south of the warband. "Then they went to the high land, through the pass."

"The tracks don't go in that direction," she said, shaking her head.

Diana stood and inspected the surrounding area. The only structure in sight was a ramshackle outbuilding at the opposite end of a pasture. It seemed on the verge of collapse, but she could see a small mountain of hay bales stacked behind it. The tracks also led straight in its direction.

"I'll bet they're hiding out in that barn over there," she said, "waiting for their new masters. Or they got here already and they're feeding them. Either way, we need to get them out."

Diana couldn't see any sign of a single, dull red trail that the Romans always left, but that only meant none of them had come through the area that night. She had learned by observation that sunlight erased the undead trails just as quickly as it killed the undead.

"We cannae let the legion retreat to the hills," Raen said as he eyed the barn. "They'll ken the caves, and have traps set."

Neac came to join them. "The lads become impatient, Seneschal. Are we to ride on, or weave our hair and gossip?"

Raen explained the situation, but nixed the chieftain's suggestion of setting fire to the barn.

"We dinnae ken if the undead are inside with the mortals."

"Our guys could stay out of sight but surround the barn," Diana suggested. "Then I can lure out the legion with a little of my yummy mortal blood. You know how much they love me."

When Diana had gone on her first patrol two weeks ago the chieftain have scoffed over using her as undead bait. Now he simply nodded and said to Raen, "I'll lead the men into the trees, and cut off their retreat. You watch over our lass."

Raen waited until the warband dismounted, secured their horses, and disappeared into the woods.

"'Twould work just as well if you would smear your blood on me, and keep your distance."

"We've talked about this," she said and drew the beautiful dagger Neac had made for her. "I'm the mortal, so I stay out of the fighting, but I can do more than just track them. Also, you guys all smell like immortal ass-kickers, which always makes them run away. I don't."

Her lover gave her a narrow look. "You enjoy baiting them."

"So much, I can't even tell you. Come on, Big

Man." She tugged the hood of her cloak over her hair. "Let's go fish for vampires."

They used what cover there was to approach the barn, until they reached a hillock. Diana shed her cloak and tied it around her waist to cover her trousers. Raen crouched and scowled as she poised the point of her blade against her fingertip, and peered around the mound before he nodded to her. She pricked herself on the dagger, squeezing her fingertip until a large bead of blood formed, and then smeared it against her neck.

Low growls came from inside the barn.

"Someone's playing my song," Diana said. She leaned over to kiss his mouth before she stood and walked toward the noise. In a sing-song voice she said, "Nothing to worry about here. I'm just a gal taking a long walk on a dark night with no one to protect me. A weak, helpless, unarmed gal. Oh, and look, I scratched myself. How clumsy of me."

Wood splintered as the door to the barn went flying across the field, and a horde of pale, black-eyed Romans came rushing out. As soon as they saw her they spread out in a circular formation, flanking her and coming around behind her to close her in.

"Hi there," she said and glanced past them

into the barn. Several mortals holding pitchforks and cudgels waited inside. "Victims with weapons. Again." She regarded the Roman stalking toward her. "By the way, how are you brainwashing them like that? Is it like a terror thing, or something you do while you're using them as a sippy cup?"

As the undead attacker showed her his fangs, a huge war hammer came flying past her and struck him in the face. The impact sent him flying into the wall of the barn, where he burst into a shower of gray ash.

Diana looked at the other undead around her. "Sorry. My boyfriend gets jealous when I talk to other guys."

Blood-curdling bellows erupted as the McDonnels charged out from the trees, which was her cue to retreat. As swords clashed she ran for the hillock, and almost reached it when two Romans came at her from either side. Raen appeared to shove her behind him, while Neac came from behind them and used his double-edged battle axe to decapitate one and then the other.

"I really want one of those now," she told the chieftain, who beamed before he charged into the fighting. "Hey, wait for–"

"No' you," Raen said, hoisting her up under his arm. He carried her back behind the mound. "You stay here," he said sternly.

"Fine, I'm staying," Diana said and watched him go. She perched on top of the hillock to keep an eye on the fighting. She'd overestimated the number of undead by twenty, which annoyed her until she saw the mortal zombies rush out the back of the barn and attack a huge pile of hay bales. "Wait a minute. Oh, damn it."

Raen had retrieved his war hammer, and he and the men were closing around the ten undead left standing in front of the barn. They couldn't see the reinforcements being helped out of the pit the hay bales had covered. Fifty more undead emerged, and Diana's blood ran cold when she saw the flare of flames. At that moment the undead fighting the clan turned and ran back into the barn.

Diana jumped down and ran, getting in front of the clansmen just in time. "Trap," she shouted, and met Raen's furious gaze. "Fifty more with torches behind the barn."

"*Stad,*" he bellowed, and all of the highlanders except one stopped in their tracks.

"Why do you dally, Brothers?" Seoc yelled. "A

glorious death awaits us all." He hefted his sword and charged toward the barn.

Raen moved like lighting, plucking the sword from the stable master and used his bulk to knock him to the ground. "Neac, *taobh*."

The chieftain echoed the order for the flanking maneuver, and the clansmen divided themselves as they streamed around the outbuilding and collided with the waiting undead. Diana knew she was supposed to take cover, but Raen was still trying to get Seoc on his feet. Suddenly the stable master hooked his arm around the big man's knees and jerked him off his feet.

"You cannae choose for me," Seoc screamed and gave Diana a wild look before he rushed at the barn.

Raen shoved himself up just as three of the legion came out and attacked the unarmed stable master, stabbing him in the sides and the front.

"Talorc, no!" Raen shouted.

Seoc smiled a little as he fell to his knees, spread out his arms, and ducked his head. One of the Romans lifted his sword and drove it into the back of his neck, killing him instantly.

Diana knew how strong her lover was, but she had never seen him go berserk. She did now.

Shouting the stable master's name, Raen ran at the trio of undead, reaching them and smashing them with his hammer before they could react. His brutal blows decapitated all three of the undead, who collapsed into piles of ash around Seoc's lifeless body. More came out of the barn, and from behind it as they fled Neac and his men. Raen became like a killing machine, thrashing his huge hammer and obliterating every Roman who came near him. Finally the last one threw himself at the big man, who split him in two with one last, brutal stroke.

Diana wanted to go to him, but something told her to hold back.

Raen stood over the dead highlander and looked up at the sky, lifting his arms toward it as he roared with pain and fury. The clan surrounded him, and held up their swords as they echoed his savage cry.

A few dazed mortals came staggering out of the barn, and Diana rushed over to lead them out of harm's way. As she did she looked at her lover, and saw the ink blazing white-hot on his face, and the tears in his eyes. Her own eyes stung as well.

It was good that Raen was immortal, because she would love him forever.

As she turned away to wrap her cloak around a trembling mortal, the old woman begged her to tell her where she was.

"You're with the McDonnels," Diana told her. "We saved your life. You're safe now."

Chapter Eighteen

TORMOD STOOD WAITING for the warband at the edge of the loch, and when Diana and Raen emerged he scowled at her. "'Tis near dawn, Red. What have you–" He fell silent as he stared at the tartan-wrapped body Raen carried. "Who?"

"Seoc Talorc," Raen said. The big man started to carry him into the stronghold, and then stopped as the Norseman took his burden. "Go gently with him," he told Tormod.

Then he turned on his heel and strode into the castle.

"Leave him, lass," Neac said as Diana started to follow. "He has to tell Lachlan about Talorc." He rested his battle axe on his shoulder. "Come and drink with us."

Diana nodded, but once in the great hall she couldn't get down more than a sip of the chieftain's whiskey. The rest of the warband also seemed uninterested in celebrating. Slowly they slipped away until only Neac remained with her.

"Ask what you will of me," the chieftain said once he drained his first tankard. "'Twill pain Aber to speak of it."

She decided to go for the big one first. "If the McDonnels are immortal, why did Seoc die?"

"We dinnae age, or grow sick, but we can be killed." He tapped the back of his neck. "A blade here, or being burned to ash, or giving ourselves to the loch again." He saw her expression. "If we dinnae change back, in time we lose ourselves in the water."

Her stomach surged, and she emptied her whiskey into his. "I think Seoc wanted the undead to kill him. I saw him bow his head, like he wanted to make it easier for them."

"What Talorc did was the only way a McDonnel can end his life with honor." Neac looked down at his whiskey before he pushed it away. "It doesnae happen often, but in these last years some of the lads have given up hope. Seoc is not the first we've lost."

Diana recalled the contempt on Seoc's face as he had spoken against her joining the clan.

"Was it because of me?"

"'Twas Evander's betrayal," Neac said flatly. "The lad took it to heart. We all did. But I thought surely in time he would…" He waved a meaty hand. "Ah, it doesnae matter now. We've lost a brother, lass, and we'll grieve for him." He patted her shoulder. "I'm to bed."

Diana carried their cups into the kitchen, and washed them in the dish basin before she hung them on the drying rack. She hadn't known Seoc, and she had never done anything to drive him to commit suicide. So why did she feel as if someone had punched a hole through her chest?

She took the stairs to the upper hall, but hesitated outside the rooms she now shared with Raen. Pressing her hand against the door, she closed her eyes for a moment as she composed herself, and then went inside.

The big man stood looking down at the fireplace, and barely glanced at her as she came in.

"I am sorry I left you as I did," he said. "I had to speak with the laird."

"I know," she said and heard the rasp of tiredness in his voice. "Is there anything I can do for you?"

His mouth twisted. "Never die."

"Right. Anything else?"

The despairing look he gave her made Diana rush to him. He caught her and held her close. The weight of his sadness seemed to bear down on him as though it were crushing him into the floor.

"Come to bed," she murmured.

Raen lifted her off her feet and carried her into their bed, where he lay with her at his side. For a long time he just stared up at the canopy, and she held onto him.

"The Talorc's tribe and mine were enemies for a long time. 'Twas why Evander and I disliked each other, I think. We couldnae let go of the old grudges, but Seoc did. He never said an unkind word to me." He pinched the bridge of his nose. "I should have guessed he would do this. I nearly did the same myself. Many times."

"What?" Diana said. She pushed away from him and rolled out of bed. "You wanted to kill yourself? Why?"

"After Bradana, I thought…no matter." He sat up and held out his hand. "Come here."

"No," she said and turned her back on him as she tried to get control of her temper. "Look, I'm sorry about your murdered wife, but you can't think like that. Ever."

"Diana," he said gently. He came up behind her, and tried to put his arms around her. "'Twas not Bradana. You cannae understand—"

"And you think you do?" She spun around and gave him a hard shove. "My God, wasn't dying once enough for you? How dare you even think about it? You have forever to *live*."

"Aye," he said quietly. "But I didnae have her to be with me, and I willnae have you."

For Diana, that was the last straw. "You know, you're right. I don't get it. I may not be older than dirt like you, but hell if I'd ever let a guy shove a sword through my neck just because I'm lonely and scared and don't have anybody to take care of me. I've always been that, and I take care of myself, just fine."

Raen held up his hands as if she were pointing her Glock at him. "I dinnae mean to fight with you."

Diana backed away before she slapped him. "Life is a gift. Right this minute there are people dying all over the world. Men, women, children, little babies. People who I'm fairly sure would give anything for more time to live. Meanwhile, your not-so-great pal Seoc throws away an immortal life tonight because, what, his jerk of a cousin embarrassed him? Please. That's not only tragic, it's disgusting. It spits in the face of every person on this planet who died and didn't want to."

He studied her face. "I heard you when you told Cailean that your mother killed herself. That her death put you in the care of others who hurt and starved you. 'Tis natural for you to abhor what Seoc did."

Diana stared at him, as all the fight went out of her.

"Sorry," she said quietly. "I shouldn't have yelled at you. Again." She dragged her hand over her hair. "I'll go sleep in the tower tonight."

Raen held out his hand. "The bed there isnae big enough for both of us. I will sleep on the floor beside it if you wish, but 'tis cold tonight, and I may catch a fever."

"You don't get sick," she muttered but took his hand and let him guide her back to their bed. "I can make you hot, if you want, but I think we're both too miserable."

"I have another idea, lass." Once he pulled

the covers over them he tugged her close. "I will hold you, and rub your back the way you like. In the morning I will kiss you awake, and then, if you willnae hate me for it, we can make each other hot."

"I can't hate you," Diana said and looked into his eyes. "I think I'm falling in love with you."

"I'll catch you with my heart when you do," he said and kissed her brow. Then smiled as he stroked his hand over her belly. "Close your eyes, and let me make you feel good."

Diana reluctantly obeyed, but instead of turning her over to get at her back he slipped his hand into her trousers. With his other hand he eased her leg up, draping it over his as he glided his fingers between her thighs.

"Touching you makes me feel better," he murmured. "You are not a soft wench, but you are here, and so pretty."

When he began circling her clit with his thumb while he pressed two fingers into her pussy, Diana lost herself in the sweet heat of the sensations.

"Raen," she whispered.

"Shhh," he said as he came around her,

pushing her onto her back and stripping off her trousers. "Let me have you."

"I want you, too," she assured him. Slowly she shifted her legs apart. "Nothing hurts when I'm with you. But I wish I could make you feel the same way."

"Be with me, and you will," he said and settled between her thighs and spread her folds.

Watching him put his mouth on her was almost as heavenly as feeling his tongue sliding against her. He didn't attack her sex or try to make her come quickly, but took his time as he kissed and licked and touched every delicate inch of her. She soon started squirming under his lips, her hips lifting and jerking as he made her want more. When he penetrated her with his tongue she fisted the bed linens, and when he sucked her clit she came with whimpering, shaking helplessness.

Diana opened her eyes to see him moving up over her, and wrapped her arms around him. "You make me forget that I was ever alone."

"Never remember it," he said and moved onto his side, holding her against him as he stroked his hand over her hair in a soothing caress. "You are with me now, my lady."

Watching his eyes, she reached for his trousers and released his engorged shaft. "You don't have to do anything, just feel this." She began stroking him gently, and sighed when he covered her breast with his hand. "Your hands feel so good on me. Let me give you some of that."

Raen's eyes darkened as he tenderly caressed her. "Always I want your touch."

It took only a few more strokes before his head fell back and he uttered a deep groan. Diana tightened her grip and increased the speed of her strokes until he began to ejaculate. Then they lay there, gazes locked, hearts pounding, and for all the sadness of the day there was a quiet joy now that made her want to weep.

"He wouldn't be mad at us for this," she said.

Raen tucked her against him. "Seoc wouldnae have minded at all. He loved bedding women, and they him." He shut his eyes. "Damn him."

"I know," she said and kissed his chin. "Let's sleep."

Chapter Nineteen

✿❀✿

THE MCDONNELS GAVE Seoc a clan burial, which Diana thought simple but rather beautiful. After Meg Talley and her maids washed the stable master's body and wrapped it in a tartan, Raen, Neac and several of the Uthars carried him out of the castle on a narrow wooden platform. They stopped at the edge of the loch, where the rest of the clan had gathered, and listened as man after man stepped forward to touch the tartan and spoke of Seoc's gallant nature, love of women, and fierce loyalty.

"Seoc was always kind to me," Kinley said as she stepped up. She looked splendid in a gown made in Lachlan's tartan pattern. "He chose a mare for me to ride who has bravely ignored my clumsiness and tolerated my lack of riding skills. Before that, during my first days with the clan, I remember how Seoc smiled whenever he saw me. Not even the laird did that." As the men quietly chuckled she pressed her slim hand to the dead man's cheek. "Good-bye, my friend."

Lachlan waited until last, and praised Seoc for the centuries he had spent breeding strong, reliable mounts for the clan, and how much of his time he had devoted to caring for them. He spoke of his mortal tribe, known to be the finest warriors among the Pritani, and how they had been among the first to join with the McDonnels to fight the Romans and protect the druids.

"Seoc Talorc died by the sword, which we must honor," the laird said, his expression growing harsh. "But he didnae have to. We might have prevented this. We all saw that he was suffering, and we did naught about it." He scanned the somber faces of the men. "We have lost too many brothers who have bowed before the sword. Let Seoc be the last."

Heads began to nod, and muttered "ayes" swept through the clan.

The castle piper began to play a mournful tune, and the McDonnels parted to make way for the laird. He went to the body, lifting it into his arms. As he walked into the loch, every McDonnel went down on one knee, and bowed their heads as Lachlan disappeared under the water.

Kinley came to stand beside Diana. "He'll take him from here out to the sea, and let him go into the northern currents. It's the Pritani custom."

"'Twould be better to do with Seoc as my people would," Tormod grumbled as he joined them.

Diana saw Raen speaking with Cailean, and neither of them looked happy. "How is putting a body in a longboat and setting it on fire before you shove it into the water better?"

The Norseman looked horrified. "Burn a boat? Are you mad? We buried our dead with weapons, and food, and slaves to serve them in the afterlife."

"Yeah, that's not better," Kinley told him. To Diana she said, "We just got word from the mainland that the Stewart laird's brother and his guards went missing overnight while out hunting. Are you and Raen still mapping the disappearances?"

She nodded. "We're starting to see a pattern. Come up to the map room, and I'll show you what we've got."

"About that manner of mapping, my lady," Tormod said to Kinley as he followed them up the stairs. "You should ken 'twas no' my doing. Red imagines herself a map maker, but she's squeamish."

"What he means is, I don't like drawing on dead animal skins," Diana corrected. "They smell and curl and they're creepy." She gestured around them as they entered. "So I'm using the room."

Kinley went to inspect the largest map Diana had drawn with one of her charcoal-sliver pencils on the white-painted stone wall.

"This is great," Kinley said. "You can just wipe off the charcoal with a rag when you need to change something." She touched the surface. "How did you bleach the rock like this?"

"It's lime, water, chalk, salt and a little flour," Diana said and grinned. "A variation on Tom Sawyer's favorite fence paint. Tormod loves it."

The Norseman snorted. "I dinnae love how it ruined my boots and trews."

"White wash, of course," Kinley said. "That's brilliant." She stepped back to take in the whole map, and her smile vanished. "These numbers by the stronghold locations, are they the people reported missing?"

"To date, yes," Diana said and came up beside her. "The pattern we found involves the circled numbers, which are nobility who have disappeared. Most of them are directly related to a laird or chieftain, usually sons or daughters, but sometimes wives or parents. All of them have gone missing over the last two weeks, and so far none of them have been recovered."

The laird's wife frowned as she started adding the numbers out loud and then turned to Diana. "We've lost fifty nobles in fourteen days? How is that even possible?"

"All the victims disappear after they leave their strongholds," Diana said. "Anyone guarding or escorting them vanishes with them, so we don't have any witnesses."

Raen came into the room carrying a pouch stuffed with tiny scrolls, which he handed to Kinley. "My lady."

He didn't have to tell her what they were, as message birds had been arriving daily from their mortal allies. The rift between the McDonnels and the druids had gone public, and while no one outside the clan and the conclave knew the actual reason for it, people were already taking sides. Raen had told Diana not to worry about it, but she suspected Bhaltair was behind it, and would keep putting pressure on the laird to surrender her to the conclave.

"That stubborn old man," Kinley muttered as she read one of the scrolls, and then tucked the pouch in her belt. "All right, back to work. What do these arrows represent, Diana?"

"The pattern that Raen and I picked up on," Diana said and went to the wall and began pointing out the disappearances in chronological order. "The nobles began vanishing here, at Clan MacLean's stronghold in the southwest. Campbell was next, then MacGregor, Menzies and now Stewart. See how they're going northeast?"

"Nobles from these clans are vanishing every two or three days, my lady," Raen said.

"Yeah, that's about right," Kinley said, her voice tight. "Lachlan and I have been working with travel times while tracking the undead. It takes two or three days to ride at night from one of these strongholds to the next. The undead are behind this. Son of a *bitch*."

Tormod produced a bottle of whiskey, and

offered it around before he took a long drink. "We can track them from Stewart's territory."

"If the pattern holds, my lady," Raen told her. He moved his hand along the next arrow, which pointed to a stronghold with no numbers written by it. "We believe Clan Gordon will be targeted next."

"I met Gordon and his wife when they got married in the spring," Kinley said as she turned away from the map and walked around the room. "The plague wiped out their families, so the earl and his wife live alone at the stronghold—for now. The countess sent me a message last month. She just got pregnant."

"We can protect them," Tormod said. "Send our lads to guard their stronghold and watch for the undead. They'll no' let the earl or his lady be taken."

"If these people *are* being abducted," Diana countered. She recalled the young mortal girl who had thrown herself on a sword to protect her undead master. "What if the undead are getting into the strongholds to brain-wash them instead of abducting them? Once the nobles are under their control, they can order them to leave their castles, and go to wherever the legion is keeping their human livestock."

"If all they want is more thralls, why target the nobles? They're much harder to get at than the average farmer," Kinley said. "It would make more sense to go after the castle guards, or servants. They wouldn't even be missed right away."

Diana had no answer for that. "We could speak with the lairds who have family missing. They may know something we don't."

"We need to talk to my husband first," Kinley said. "We should bring Neac and Cailean in on this, too." She touched the message pouch. "And maybe this will finally convince the old man to give us a break."

Later that night they met with the laird, the chieftain and the druid in the map room, where Raen and Diana related their pattern theory.

"I know it seems like a stretch," Diana told him. "But in my time we look for similarities or connections between victims. It helps us learn more about the offender, establish their motives and methods of operation, and sometimes allows us to even anticipate what they'll do next. We may not know why these people are being taken, but if we can stop the next incident, we may find out."

"I can tell you," the laird said. "MacLean is the king's *mormaer* in the western territories. He has authority over all the lesser clans. Campbell's son wed the king's daughter, and sired five of his grandchildren, so he 'tis regarded as a member of the royal family. McGregor has the largest armory in the country, and supplies the royal guard and garrison with all their weapons. Menzies manages trade with towns in Britannia, and Stewart is one of the most valuable battle generals in Scotland. All of these lairds are men important to the king."

"But the undead didn't take any of the lairds," Tormod said. "Why leave them behind?"

"All the lairds are too well-guarded," Cailean told him. "Taking their kin hostage is easier, and still forces the lairds to do their bidding."

"Gordon's lady is who I'd take," Tormod said. When everyone glared at him he shrugged. "A pregnant wife is ever dearly loved, and two hostages in one."

"The countess is with child?" Cailean asked abruptly.

If Kinley hadn't known better, the druid

might have passed for one of the undead himself. His face had gone pale.

"Aye," Neac told him. "So she has messaged to Kinley."

As Cailean took some moments to absorb the information, Kinley took hold of her husband's hand.

"We can't let them grab the countess," she said. When she saw Diana's expression, she said, "She's a beautiful woman, so the undead won't use her just for blood. They'll rape her until she miscarries. If she survives that, she'll never recover."

Without thinking Diana reached out to Raen, who put an arm around her shoulders. "We've got two days to get in front of this. We should move the Gordons out of their stronghold, and stash them somewhere safe. Then dress me up like the countess, and use me as bait again."

"Aye," Lachlan said as his expression turned thoughtful and his gaze shifted to Raen. "But you'll need a husband."

Chapter Twenty

A DAY LATER the laird left Clan Gordon's stronghold with the earl and his countess, leaving behind a hundred McDonnels to guard Raen and Diana while they posed as the nobles.

"Keep your hammer and the lieutenant close to you," Lachlan said as he walked out of the castle with Raen to the waiting carriage. "The undead cannae enthrall her if they must first go through you." He glanced at the Gordon's laird, who held his lovely wife in his arms as if he never intended to release her. "Neac and Kinley have gone to the druid settlement. She hopes to persuade Bhaltair to end this quarrel between us by telling him of the work you and Diana have done to safeguard our mortal allies."

"As your wife would say, dinnae hold your breath." Raen almost bowed before he caught himself. "I forget we pretend to be equals."

"'Tis good to see you as a laird. You have the head and the heart for it, Brother." The laird clasped his forearm before he climbed into the carriage with the nobles.

Raen checked the number of exterior guards and their stations, and inspected once more the castle's fortifications for flaws. Gordon's father had begun work on his stronghold during a time of constant conflict, placing it atop a high outcropping of rock, and clearing the land around to remove anything that might provide cover to advancing troops. Instead of a moat the old laird had lined the sloped approaches on all sides with pit and snare traps, and acres of sharpened stakes projecting up from the ground. Every battlement and gate passage was pocked with murder holes, through which fire, arrows and even spears could be dropped on the heads of invaders. With fifty men guarding the exterior, and twice as many McDonnels occupying the interior, it seemed impossible for any undead to infiltrate the place.

Yet they had done so at five other strongholds that had been equally well-defended. How were

they getting inside? And how was he to keep
Diana safe from them?

Raen nodded to the gate sentries as he
returned inside, where the laird's steward stood
waiting with a long-handled brush, the Gordon
tartan, and a pinched look on his face.

"My lord," the steward said, and handed him
a message scroll. "This came for you. You must
dress for the evening meal."

He glanced down at the fine clothes he had
borrowed from Gordon. "I am dressed."

The shorter man leaned close and said in a
bare whisper. "Our laird doesnae wear the same
clothes from dawn to dusk. Also, you must wear
the tartan. Always. 'Tis a mark of your position."

"'Tis no' my position," Raen told him, and
sighed as the man scurried around him to ply his
brush over his garments. "I will remain as I am."
He looked around for Diana. "Have you seen
my lady?"

"I believe she is being dressed."

With a self-satisfied smirk the man stalked off.

Raen shook his head and opened the scroll,
which had been sent by Neac. The chieftain wrote
that he and Kinley had not found Bhaltair at the
druid settlement. Rather than travel back to Dun

Aran, they would spend the night there and try to convince the other conclavists that Diana should stay with the clan.

Raen knew Diana thought she was helping the clan by acting as bait for the undead, but he hated it. Each time she did so, she risked her life. He knew how fragile mortals could be. All it would take was one undead to get to her, and then—

"Can anyone else be the bait?"

Raen looked up from the message to see Diana walking very slowly down the staircase. For a moment he forgot to breathe. She looked like something from a dream in the soft lavender gown she wore. The countess's delicate silver and amethyst jewels glinted from her fingers, throat and ears, and thick braids of her golden red hair had been arranged like a crown on her head. He went to stuff the message in his pocket, and realized the earl's trews and coat didn't possess any.

"You look like a countess," he told her. "Also, Kinley is staying at the druid settlement with Neac tonight, and there are no other women in the house but maids."

She squinted at him. "Why are you looking at me like that?"

Because he was in love with her and the

thought of losing her was slowly gutting him. Yet someday he would, and he could tell her none of that.

"I have never seen you in a dress."

"Did you know that it's made of wool, and weighs about twenty pounds? I'm also wearing more underwear than a Mormon. My shoes are so tight I can't feel my toes. Plus there are pins in my hair—huge, sharp, scary pins—that feel like they're about to perform ad hoc brain surgery on me." She winced her way over to him. "Why am I not getting hazard pay for this?"

He bent down to kiss her lips. "We dinnae pay you."

"If this keeps up, that's going to change." She hobbled over to the nearest chair, sat down and tugged off her too-small slippers. "Ah. So much better. I'm wearing my boots under the dress. No arguments. No one will see them, and I can't fight if I'm crippled."

One of the housemaids hurried over to bob before Raen and said to Diana, "Lieutenant, the evening meal awaits in the dining hall." She immediately froze. "I mean, my lady."

"Not a lady, sweetie." Diana handed her the

slippers. "Burn these. Please. The countess will thank me."

Raen escorted her barefoot into the dining hall, where the enormous table had been set for two at one end. Another half of the table had been filled with roasted haunches, stuffed poultry, fragrant breads, artfully-arranged vegetables and fruits, soups and sauces.

Diana went up to one of the guards. "Did you guys invite an army to have dinner with us, and forget to mention it?"

The man's lips twitched. "No, my lady. The laird had planned to dine with his stewards and overseers tonight. In the haste to remove him and his wife, we didnae send word to the kitchens."

"No one told the cook. Gotcha." Diana glanced around the room, and said to Raen, "We're not wasting all this food. Let's send for some more dishes, and the guards can eat with us."

Raen considered explaining mortal clan protocol to her, but Diana had little respect for rank or privilege. Being starved in childhood had also made her particularly sensitive to the waste of food.

"You heard the lieutenant, lads. Take a seat."

While the Gordon clansman at first remained stiff and silent at the table, Diana started talking about riding Treun, and how the gelding wouldn't spook, even when she had slid off the horse's hindquarters to land between his back hooves.

"All I got was a tail in my face," she said as she passed a bowl of cream to the guard beside her. "Which of course I grabbed, and yanked, and Treun just made this disgusted sound." She imitated the horse by blowing air through her lips.

The guards looked startled, and then began to grin and chuckle. Soon they traded stories about their own mounts, which sparked a discussion on the merits of highland-bred horses versus the muscular destriers favored by the Spanish and French.

By the time the meal ended Raen felt melancholy as well as miserable. Seoc would have loved to be a part of this night. Why had he agreed to this ruse? He had survived losing Bradana, but if anything happened to Diana, he wouldn't want to.

The door opened as an older woman in an apron and cap came in carrying a huge silver platter of pastries decorated with berries and flowers. "I have your favorite sweet tonight, my la—" She stopped and stared at Diana before looking around the table. "Who are you? Where is our laird and lady? Why do the men sit with you?"

"Because standing would make it harder for them to eat," Diana said.

"The laird's steward will explain everything to you, Mistress," Raen said as he stood and took the platter. She looked up at him, squealed and fled. "The meal was much enjoyed," he called after her as she ran out of the room.

"We need to get some of her recipes for Meg," Diana said as she picked up a large round pastry covered with tiny rosebuds. "I love cake." She bit into it with a sigh.

"Best take yours now, lads," Raen told the guards.

After they finished the sweets Diana said good-night to the guards, and accompanied Raen up to the laird's bedchamber. He stood by as a maid prepared her for bed, and then dismissed the servant.

"I think it's going to be tonight," Diana said as she placed the countess's jewelry in an ornate chest. "Remember, don't kill the undead. They have to escape so I can track them to where they've been hiding out during the day. It could also be where they're holding the other hostages." She glanced at him. "Stop looking at me like that. It's the plan. I'll be fine."

"And what if you're no'?" he demanded. "What am I to do if you're hurt, or taken, or bitten by those bastarts?"

"Hey," she said and hurried over to him. "I've got you with me. You're my bodyguard. You make me safer than anyone in Scotland."

Raen drew her into his arms. "You'd be safer back at Dun Aran." He covered her mouth with his, kissing her until they both trembled, and then tucked his short dagger in her hand. "Go to bed, then, Wife."

With a grumpy sound Diana stomped over to the bed. "I should strip and touch myself in front of you." She perked up. "You know, we could both do that until the undead show up."

Raen pointed to the bed.

"Spoilsport," she said but flopped down and heaved a sigh.

Raen spent the rest of the night standing opposite the laird's bed while watching Diana pretend to sleep. An hour before dawn she finally dozed off, but he didn't try to wake her. The undead would have to be mad to strike so close to sunrise. Once the sky outside the windows brightened with sunlight he gave into his own weariness, and tucked his hammer beside the bed before he joined her.

Diana murmured something as she turned and snuggled against him, and he closed his eyes.

He liked sharing a bed with his cop. When he had been married, he and Bradana had only had the meadow or the orchards. They had never once shared a bed or a home, but he had promised her that they would someday. After her death the guilt he'd felt had made him avoid women altogether for years, until Neac had talked him into paying a visit to a brothel on the mainland he favored.

Raen hadn't liked bedding the young mortal wench Neac had chosen for him, but she looked nothing like Bradana. Feeling no desire for her, he had been unable to finish for a long time, which had pleased her a great deal. As soon as she fell asleep he had dressed and left the brothel, hurrying out to the trees to empty his belly on the ground.

Most of the clan paid for their pleasures. The women always welcomed them for their prowess and their generous purses, and it prevented attachments from forming. Raen continued going to the brothel occasionally to relieve his needs, but he always returned to Dun Aran feeling empty and even more alone. Then Diana had come, with her easy grin, and her sharp mind, and her endless courage. He no longer wondered why his spirit had chosen to mark her as his. She had made him and his battered heart hers.

Raen felt himself streaming through currents, and opened his eyes to see shafts of sunlight illuminating the dark water. Water lily vines cascaded around him as he swam for shore. Then he saw a flutter of pale lavender fabric, and looked down to see Bradana's swollen, lifeless face staring up at him from a tangle at the bottom of the pond. Even as he swam down to her he knew it couldn't be his sweet wife. He'd buried her in their meadow fifty years back.

Her eyes lightened to match her dress, and suddenly she was Diana, fighting off the undead who came from all directions, tearing at her dress and dragging her down to drown her.

"*No*," he muttered.

Raen opened his eyes to darkness and reached for his hammer. He looked over at Diana who lay struggling under Gordon's steward. The man had black eyes now, and fangs sprouting from his mouth. Without hesitation Raen swung his hammer at the steward's head, splitting it in two. The undead shrieked as his face changed. For a brief moment, he shifted back into his own form and then disintegrated all over Diana.

She rolled off the bed and headed to the closed drapes, but was struck by a cudgel-wielding maid and fell to the floor. One of the laird's guards grabbed her and dragged her to her feet, bearing his fangs as he wrenched back her head.

Raen hurled himself at the undead, knocking him away from Diana and into a cabinet. Wood splintered around them as they grappled, and the maid screamed as she tried to get between them. He shoved the wench away and moved back, raising his hammer as the guard shifted form. Two more guards rushed at them, and Raen dimly heard Diana shout his name, but he could not stop himself.

A moment later ash filled the air and the maid fell to her knees and began to weep.

Raen turned to see Diana staggering to her feet, and dropped his hammer as he went to seize her by the arms.

"Were you bitten? Did they touch you?"

"No, and they didn't brainwash me, either." She tugged herself out of his grasp and opened the curtains, and then looked at the maid, who was sobbing into her hands. "At least she's still human. Why didn't you let them go?"

He peered at her. "What?"

"We were going to let them escape, remember? So I could track them?" When he didn't reply Diana dragged her hand through her hair and looked around at the dust-covered floor. "Well, at least we know how they're getting inside. They're killing the guards and taking on their shape." She gave him a wan smile. "Thanks for the save."

"Dinnae thank me." The words left his mouth with harsh coldness to them, but it couldn't be helped. "You were not safe with me next to you. If I hadnae woken they would have taken you from the bed. You would be enthralled by now."

"We didn't know they would attack during the day," she countered. "They must be getting in the houses at night and waiting until daylight when everyone's guard is down. We can use that information for the next time."

She was already thinking about risking her life

again. She would keep putting herself in danger, and no matter how careful he was, he couldn't protect her. She would end up dead.

"There will no' be a next time," he grated. "You are a mortal, Diana, and you are no' safe here. *I* cannae keep you safe."

"Look, you're just shaken up. It's okay, and so am I." She held out her hand. "Come here."

"No, Lieutenant." Raen stepped back out of her reach. "Bhaltair is right. You dinnae belong here. You have to go back to your time."

Chapter Twenty-One

❧❦❧

"WELL, TREUN, WE'VE got a little problem," Diana said as she reined in the gelding and scanned the horizon, which at the far north showed a glimmer of ocean. "I don't know where the hell we are, but it looks like we're running out of Scotland."

Now that she had ridden for most of the day her temper had simmered down, which made it easier to think straight. She probably shouldn't have told Raen to drop dead, especially since that was basically impossible. Nor should she have borrowed the laird's clothes, walked out of the stronghold and taken off on her horse without saying good-bye to anyone. Raen had left her to stew, while he went to send a message to Lachlan

about the failed abduction, and his recommenda-
tion that they boot her back to the twenty-first
century.

Diana didn't need Raen to hold her hand, or
protect her, or give her permission to do her job.
She sure as hell wasn't waiting around for Bhaltair
to show up and shove her back to the future
through a sacred oak grove.

She'd originally planned to go to Lamont's
stronghold, where she'd check on the earl and his
daughter, and maybe stay long enough to cool off
and figure out what to do next. Then she'd picked
up a mortal trail with an odd reddish tinge to it,
which merged with another, and another, until she
was following hundreds of converged trails. They
wound around towns and villages, through
pastures and hills, and even pooled around an
abandoned ruin before following a very old road
to the north. And while the road appeared
neglected and nearly overgrown by weeds, Diana
saw several new sets of wheel ruts following the
undead trails.

Narrow ruts, which were the exact type left by
the carriages used by nobles.

Now that she was about to run into the ocean
Diana suspected the odd trails would diverge in a

hundred different directions, but found instead that they took an abrupt turn and crossed the expansive fields surrounding a huge, ancient stronghold, where they ended.

Diana rode on to a nearby village, where she dismounted and led Treun to water him at a public trough. The locals eyed her with visible unease, but no one spoke to her or challenged her presence. Considering she was a woman dressed as a man and wearing a Gordon tartan, she thought that more than a little strange.

Working off a hunch, she walked over to a boy who was waving a twig around while pretending to ride a larger stick like a horse.

"Fair day to you, Master. Might a lad like you help a fellow warrior?"

The boy screwed up his face as he inspected her. "I'm no' a warrior, and you're a wench."

Just her luck, she'd picked the brightest kid in the village. "True enough. Can you tell me who owns that big castle with the stone wall around it?"

"Ermindale belongs to the laird," he said as he bounced around her on his stick. "Everything here does."

"Has the laird had a lot of new visitors lately?" When the boy nodded, she smiled. "Did they come here in carriages?"

"I didnae see them, but I heard them. They come at night." The boy poked her arm with his twig. "Do you think they killed the magic folk?"

Diana kept her expression bland and shrugged. "Do you think they did?"

"I dinnae ken. My da says they did. He's afeared of them." The boy gave her a solemn look. "They took my mam to the castle to work one night. 'Tis been a moon and she's no' come back."

"Rabbie, there ye are," an old woman said as she came up and herded the boy away, keeping her eyes averted from Diana. "Come inside now, lad. I've made your supper."

As Diana walked back to Treun she noticed that all of the villagers who had been working outside were now retreating into their cottages and barns. She heard bars dropping into place as they barricaded their doors, as if they thought she might try to come after them.

A good cop didn't jump to conclusions, but this one was practically jumping up and down on her head.

She rode around Ermindale to look for a

vantage point close to the stronghold, and found one on a hill above the castle's sadly neglected gardens. She hobbled Treun in a pasture of thick, lush grass by a stream, and then climbed the hill and found a niche where she could watch the house without being observed. Nothing she saw at first seemed out of the ordinary. Servants came and went as they worked, guards patrolled, and sentries kept to their posts. To alleviate her boredom she counted the number of patrols, and noted how often the sentries were relieved. Things got even busier as the sun set. All around the outer walls torches were lit by the sentries before they retreated into the castle.

Diana watched an elderly man wearing all black stride out into the gardens, and held her breath when she saw he was accompanied by a tall, gray-haired man wearing a red tartan. They were followed by a group of well-dressed men and women who seemed to hang on their every word, which she was too far away to hear.

They could be visitors, and the kid in the village simply had an overworked mother and an overactive imagination, but Diana still felt dread knot up her gut. All the men in the group were wearing tartans of differing colors and patterns, which meant different clans. All the women looked pale in the torchlight.

Another man came out of the castle, stopped in front of the gray-haired laird, and slapped his arm across his chest armor. He wore a flowing red cloak over Roman battle armor, and seemed to be reporting to the laird and the old man. Then the laird removed his tartan, revealing his own armor, while the new shift of sentries assumed their posts outside the stronghold.

The sentries wore clan clothing, but had skin so white it looked like they'd been carved from plaster, and eyes that were the same shade of reptilian black as the undead Diana had fought.

Her gut had been absolutely right. The legion had taken over Ermindale.

Diana crept down the hill and retrieved the gelding. Carefully walking Treun across the stream and away from the castle, she considered her options. It would take too long to ride back to Gordon's stronghold, and Raen had probably already left to look for her. She was closer to Lamont's, and from her patrols with the clan she knew what roads to take to get there. The earl also had couriers. She could send a report directly to Dun Aran from there.

"I hope you had a decent break, pal," Diana said to Treun as she mounted the horse. "Because there won't be any more tonight."

Knowing the horse couldn't gallop the entire distance without dropping from exhaustion, Diana kept her mount at a steady pace while she thought about everything she had seen at Ermindale. If the clan was to attack, they'd have to go in the morning, when the undead would be unable to spot them approaching or come out and fight. Assuming the nobles being held there were all brainwashed, they'd have to lure them out somehow and get them contained so they didn't try to protect their undead masters. The locals were obviously scared out of their minds, so they wouldn't offer much help. Maybe she'd consult with the earl's daughter on how to best infiltrate the castle, seeing as Nathara was already an expert on how to get out of one unnoticed.

"What we need, Treun, is a great big Trojan laundry basket," Diana joked, and then tugged on the reins as she saw the sunrise glimmering behind the silhouette of the earl's gatehouse. "Boy, you really can trot. Extra oats for you when we get home."

She dismounted and led the tired gelding up

to the castle entry, and then stopped as she saw a man in druid's robes standing just outside it.

"I need to speak with the laird right away," she told them, and peered at the druid, who pushed back his hood. "Cailean. What are you doing here?"

"I have been looking for you, Lieutenant. So has Master Aber." He gestured for one of the laird's sentries to take Treun. "I must speak with you on an urgent matter. Will you walk with me?"

"Uh, okay, sure." She followed him past the gatehouse and into the woods surrounding the estate. "How did you know I'd be here?"

He shrugged. "We have our ways."

That was druid-speak for classified info, so Diana asked, "Did Raen tell you about this morning? Long story short, the undead are posing as the guards and having enthralled household staff let them inside to get at the nobles. They can also do it during the day."

"We ken." He went around a large oak into a small circular clearing, and then stopped and turned to her. "I am sorry about this, Lieutenant. As I have said, I have always liked you."

Diana felt someone else coming up behind her, and guessed why he'd lured her away from

Lamont's stronghold. But instead of surprise or anger, a strange familiarity filled her. She'd known it couldn't last.

"How about you, old guy?" she asked. "Still nursing that grudge?"

"I have forgiven you for harming me," Bhaltair said as he came around her, his eyes cold and his expression dark with some tightly-leashed emotion. "We are all grateful for what you have done for the clan and druid kind, Mistress Burke."

"No, you're not," she said simply and glanced down to see the center of the clearing glowing faintly. "But I bet it'll feel good when you drop-kick me back to my time, huh?" She didn't wait for him to answer, but instead turned to Cailean. "Tell Raen this: I'm sorry, I love him, and I'll be okay."

The younger druid gave her a pained smile. "Safe journey, Diana."

Safe journey? It'd be anything but. She'd be better off with the un—

"Wait," she exclaimed. "I have to tell you." But Bhaltair had already raised a hand. "*No*. The clan needs to go to Ermin—"

Something shoved Diana forward onto the glowing spot, which sucked her down into the ground and through the long, curving tunnel of trees. This time she didn't feel any fear. She knew what was waiting for her on the other end. She only wished she hadn't left Raen without saying good-bye, but she doubted she would have been able to say it without breaking down.

Maybe this way was better.

It was almost painless.

The world brightened around her as the tunnel emptied her out onto the ground, and she sat up to see fresh crime scene tape wound around the trees. The tape seemed to be sparkling, too, or maybe it was the brightness of the day. The sky looked as pale as milk around the huge orb of the sun, and Diana closed her eyes against the stabbing pain that looking at it inflicted.

She had gone on one final adventure. She'd found Kinley, and fallen in love. That didn't hurt. That was every last wish, fulfilled to the max.

The pain didn't go away, but ballooned, pressing on the sides of her skull from within. Soon she was curled over and holding her head to keep it from exploding.

"Hey, lady, are you all right?" a voice said. A bearded man appeared over her, and then knelt down beside her. "Are you hurt? Let me see. I know some first aid."

"I'm not...hurt. I'm...sick." Diana could hear how she slurred the words, and knew she didn't have much time left. "Call. Ambulance."

"Honey, call nine-one-one," the bearded man said to someone else as he rolled Diana over onto her side. "Tell them she's having a seizure." A woman's voice spoke, and then he said, "I don't know. Maybe it's epilepsy."

No, Einstein, she thought as the shakes stopped, and her vision darkened to black. *It's an inoperable brain tumor.*

The oak grove seemed to shimmy around Diana, and then her body convulsed as the time bomb that had been ticking in her head for the last two years finally went off.

Chapter Twenty-Two

❧❧

RAEN PERSONALLY SEARCHED all of Gordon's land for Diana before returning to Dun Aran in hopes of finding her there. He knew he had been a fool to speak to her out of fear instead of love, and he would convince her to forget his irrational proposal. Even if it was safer for her in her time, he knew he could not live without her in his.

At the castle Diana was nowhere to be found, and when the clan's horses were brought back from the mainland, Treun was not among them. Raen spoke to every member of the warband that had gone with him and Diana to the Gordon's castle. Two clansmen reported seeing Diana, dressed in the laird's clothes, saddle and ride off on her gelding.

"I saw her looking to the ground," one of the men said. "As she does when she's tracking."

That she would go in search of the undead by herself terrified Raen, who went to his rooms to pack what he needed for his journey. She did not know Scotland or the mortals of this time. She would give that away the first time she spoke to anyone. Being a woman dressed like a man would make every clan suspicious of her. The ignorant and often superstitious villagers might think her a witch. After dark she could be captured and enthralled by any undead who desired her.

Raen went down to the great hall, where he saw Lachlan and Kinley talking with Neac. For the first time since the awakening he didn't feel any interest in whatever clan business they were discussing. All he could think of was his woman, out there alone somewhere, furious with him and unaware that she'd put herself in grave danger.

As soon as he saw him Neac hurried over. "You dinnae have to search for Diana," the chieftain said.

"I have naught to do but that," Raen said, and went to the laird. "I drove her away. I am going after her. I dinnae ken when I will return."

Lachlan offered him a message scroll and said, "Have a look, lad."

Raen took it and read it, but the words made no sense. "Lamont wishes to keep Treun for his daughter? Why would he…oh, fack me. She's there now? Why didnae you say before?"

"She's not there." The laird turned over the paper to show him the rest of the message. "Lamont says she was taken from the gatehouse by a druid."

The air in Raen's lungs turned to lead as his gaze shifted to Cailean, who sat by the hearth and was staring into the flames. *A druid.* He felt his body harden as if he were about to go into battle. *Dinnae kill him, no' yet.* He strode over, seized the front of the druid's robe, and dragged him out of the chair.

"What did you do to Diana?" Raen demanded, lifting him until his boots dangled above the floor.

"Master Aber," the druid managed to say. Sweat popped out on his pale face. "You must ken I wouldnae ever… I cannae… Please put me down."

Raen had never been a man to inflict harm on the helpless, and he had always had great respect for the magic folk. None of that mattered to him in this moment.

"Answer me now, and true, or I will put you down in the facking fire and watch you burn."

Cailean gulped. "'Twas Master Flen. I am his acolyte. I've no choice but to obey him. He discovered where the lieutenant would be, and bid me go there with him. To enforce the ruling, 'tis all."

Raen dropped him to the floor, but Tormod immediately stepped in and backed the druid up against the wall.

"You helped Bhaltair send Red back to her time? *She's clan.*"

"We will deal with the druids later, Viking," Lachlan said. "Now we must retrieve Diana. We can use the sacred grove here to reach her. Cailean, can Kinley safely pass through the grove now that she is immortal?"

The druid nodded quickly. "The resurrection spell healed all of her wounds, as it did the clan's. They willnae return in any time, as yours didnae when you last went through the grove, my lord. But my lady, surely it would be better if…" His voice trailed off as he saw how everyone was glaring at him. "Or no'."

"You need to deal with the undead," Kinley said to the laird, "not to mention Bhaltair, so I'm not taking you with me this time. But trust me, I'll be back, and I'll have our cop."

Lachlan kissed his wife, and nodded to Raen. "Go."

"I am coming with you," Tormod said, taking down an ax from a weapons rack.

He paused to glance at Lachlan who gave him a nod.

"Fine, but you can't bring that," Kinley said. She turned to address them both. "When we arrive you have to let me do all the talking. Also, you can't freak out over things. If we have to go into the city after Diana, it's going to be really scary, but you just have to stay calm."

"I dinnae care about your city," Raen told her flatly. "I go there only for my lady."

Kinley touched his arm. "Let's move."

They left the stronghold and hurried out across the glen to the grove where Diana had originally crossed over from her time. Raen felt something very old and powerful in the air as soon as Kinley entered the grove.

"Hold onto me while we're crossing," she warned them as she stretched out her hands. "And don't let go. I don't want to lose either of you to the space between time. Ready?"

"No," Tormod said and wrapped his arm around hers. "Yes."

Raen held her free hand, and Kinley stepped forward into the center of the grove. The ground beneath them shook, and then vanished.

The last time Raen had made this journey he had been dying. Now he was fully awake and aware, and felt the immense power hurtling them through eight centuries to Diana's world, and it seemed a good time to entreat the gods. *I know 'tis my fault, and I shouldnae have driven her from me. I will accept any punishment you wish. Please, take us to her.*

A heartbeat later they dropped out of the portal, and Raen found himself standing between two oak trees in front of the smoothest, most perfect curtain wall he had ever seen.

"Okay," Kinley said, looking around them. "We're at San Diego General instead of Horsethief Canyon. Oh, my god. I think this is a portal." She touched one of the oaks. "Or it was."

"You have strange names for things." Tormod said as he stared up at the huge building. "Is this Diana's stronghold?" He turned his head to gape at a pretty young blonde in a tank top and shorts. "Oh, tell me that wench 'tis her sister."

"She doesnae have blood kin," Raen told him, and felt another stab of guilt. He had been so adamant about keeping her safe that he hadn't considered how miserable she might be in her time, where she only had her work.

"This is a hospital, a place where sick people are brought to be healed," the laird's wife said, frowning. "The portal must have brought us here for a reason. Maybe Diana got hurt when she was forced through by Bhaltair. Come on."

Tormod stared at everything they passed inside the hospital, but Raen only scanned the faces of every woman within sight. "Kinley, she is no' here."

"We'll check with patient information," she told him, and walked up to a huge, curved object behind which mortals were sitting and working on strange devices. "Hi, can you tell me if Diana Burke is a patient here? She would have been admitted last night."

The woman checked one of the lighted gadgets and nodded. "She's in intensive care, room four-bee. Are you family?"

"Yes, I'm her sister," Kinley said, and pointed

to Raen. "This is her husband, and her brother."
As the woman stared at all three of them she
added, "We were just at a cosplay convention.
We're immortal highlanders. Don't we look
authentic?"

"Uh-huh," the woman said, and handed
Kinley three slips of paper with large Vs on them.
"It's about time some family showed up. Intensive
Care is on the seventh floor. Visitation is restricted
to thirty minutes, and you can't leave anything in
the room."

Kinley had them walk into a large metal box,
which jerked and hummed as it rose, and dinged
when it stopped. When they walked out they were
in another, new place crowded with mortals and
more gadgets and bedchambers. From there she
guided them through the crowded corridor to a
room where the bed had been draped.

Raen could smell Diana, and jerked aside the
curtains, only to freeze. "My lady?"

All of her glorious mane was gone, and in its
place was a flimsy, short cap of thin, fragile-
looking hairs. Her body now looked too thin and
fragile, and her eyes appeared sunken and cloudy.
The left side of her face drooped, and she didn't
react at all to their presence.

"She can't speak," a kind voice said, and a woman dressed in white entered the room. "Ms. Burke had several grand mal seizures, and then a stroke when she reached the ER. I'm afraid it's common with her type of brain tumor."

The woman took hold of Diana's limp hand and pressed her fingers across her wrist as she stared at her own bracelet.

"My sister never told us about her illness," Kinley said carefully. "I think she didn't want to worry us. Will she be having surgery?"

"Oh, my dear, I'm so sorry. There's nothing we can do for your sister now but make her comfortable." The woman adjusted one of the tubes attached to Diana's arm. "When you're finished visiting, we would like to discuss transferring Ms. Burke to a hospice facility."

Kinley nodded, waited until the woman left, then turned to Raen.

"I can't take us back from here. We have to move her to where we crossed over, between the oak trees." She glanced over her shoulder at the door. "All right, this will have to be quick and dirty." She turned to Tormod. "I need you by the elevator. If anyone tries to stop us, you knock them out."

"The elevator is the metal box with the glowing discs?"

Kinley nodded and the Viking slipped out of the room.

"I'll be right back. Stay here with her," Kinley said, and followed Tormod.

Raen gently picked up Diana's hand to hold it between his. "What I said to you before we parted was a lie. I can keep you safe. All you must do is stay with me." He leaned over to kiss her cool brow. "You must, you ken, for you bear my mark." He turned her palm up to kiss it, and saw the jag of ink had vanished. "I forgot that you are as you were before you came to Dun Aran. It doesnae matter. You are mine."

A spark jumped from his face to her palm, and etched the mark again.

Diana opened her eyes, and one side of her mouth curled up. "Ouch."

At that moment Kinley came back into the room pushing a chair with large wheels that contained a pile of garments. She handed Raen a large white coat.

"Put this on," she ordered and then donned one herself. "Once I disconnect her from the equipment, I need you to put her in the wheel-

chair. Then we're going to take her to the elevator." She looked down at Diana and smiled. "Hey,
lady. You didn't think you'd get out of the clan
that easy, did you?"

Raen watched as the laird's wife quickly
removed all of the wires and tubes from Diana's
body, and then eased his arms under her and
lifted her from the bed. She felt as weightless as a
child, and once he placed her in the chair Kinley
covered her with a thin blanket.

"Don't look at anyone, and walk normally,"
she said before she opened the door.

She looked left and right, and then pushed
Diana out of the room.

The mortals working around the rooms didn't
notice them. But as they drew close to the elevator, where Tormod was standing, another woman
wearing white stopped and peered at Diana, and
then Kinley.

"Where are you taking this patient?" the
woman demanded.

"Downstairs," Kinley said, sounding bored as
she went to press the button on the wall between
the metal boxes.

"But she isn't scheduled for–"

The woman squealed as Tormod turned her

around, lifted her up, and kissed her until she clutched his neck.

The doors to the elevator opened, and Kinley rolled Diana inside.

"You are very comely," the Norseman said. "I wish I could bring you back for me." But he lowered the dazed woman to the ground, and darted into the elevator just before the doors closed. When he saw Kinley's face he shrugged. "I couldnae hit her over the head. She is a healer."

Raen held onto Diana's thin hand as the elevator descended, and then pushed the wheelchair out and walked rapidly toward the clear doors. He heard some of the mortals calling to them, but didn't stop until they were outside. He lifted Diana out of the chair, wrapped the blanket around her and carried her to the space between the two oaks.

Kinley and Tormod joined them, and the laird's wife smiled down at Diana as she tucked her arms through the men's. "Time to go home."

Raen held onto Diana tightly as they fell into the portal's tunnel, and felt her growing heavier in his arms as they made the journey back to Skye. When he looked down at her, he saw her hair thicken and grow out in long, shining waves of golden red. Her face grew symmetrical and smooth, and her eyes brightened as she met his gaze.

The next moment they were standing in the oak grove, surrounded by red deer who stood and watched them with big dark eyes, before returning to their grazing.

Carefully Raen lowered Diana to the ground, and looked all over her. Seeing her restored to herself made his throat lock up.

Diana raised her hands to touch her head. "I have hair again." She uttered a little laugh. "I had to wear a wig for like a year." She looked at Kinley and Tormod. "Thank you. You just saved my life."

The laird's wife hugged her. "You're my sister in any time."

Diana turned to Tormod. "You blew your chance to get rid of me for good."

"Aye." He scowled. "Dinnae ever do that again. If you do I will have to kill many druids, and they will come back and curse me or feed my soul to the dogs of the gods."

"Come on, Viking," Kinley said. "Let's go tell my husband we've got our tracker back before *he* kills many druids."

Raen waited until the pair left.

"I had a dream of finding Bradana in the pond, that night we were at Gordon's stronghold. Her face changed to yours, and the undead were drowning you. When I woke up and saw them attacking you, 'twas as if I'd had an omen. That was why I spoke to you so coldly. I wanted you to go back so you would live." He hesitated. "Why didnae you tell Bhaltair that going back would kill you?"

"He wouldn't care," she said quietly. "But I should have told you." She shook her head a little. "I've been hiding this tumor for a very long time. I intended to keep my job up to the very last second. I also wasn't sure coming to your time cured me, and I didn't want you to think that was the only reason I wanted to stay." She paused and looked at the ground. "Maybe it was in the beginning."

"This was why you were angry with me after Seoc died," Raen said and touched her cheek. "'Twas not about your mother. 'Twas about you."

"I kept my condition secret for as long as I could. I lied to my boss and told her that I was cancer-free. But I fought it, Raen. I tried medication, chemo, radiation and even something called alternating electric field therapy. For that one they stuck an electrode on my scalp and made me carry around a thing that constantly zapped the tumor." She rubbed her head. "Nothing worked. When I crossed over, I had only a few weeks left to live, so when Kinley told me she'd been healed… well, it gave me some real hope. Then you and I went for a swim, and the ink started to fly, and I thought, maybe I could have it all. My life and you." As she looked up at him, her hand pressed down over his heart. "So I've got the life back."

"And me," he said, smiling down at her as he covered her hand with his. "You'll no' be rid of me as easy as that."

Unshed tears glittered in her violet eyes as Raen bent down and slowly kissed her. She held onto him tightly, her soft lips melding into his, and her spiced-honey scent filling his head. But after a long moment, she drew back.

"There's one more thing," she said. "I know where the nobles and the legion are."

Chapter Twenty-Three

D IANA FELT ALMOST embarrassed by the hearty welcome she received as soon as she and Raen returned to the stronghold. Every guard greeted her and clasped arms with her, and as soon as she entered the kitchens Meg Talley embraced her like a long-lost daughter. In the great hall Neac grabbed her and gave her a bone-cracking squeeze before passing her around like a big doll to the Uthars, who did the same.

Finally she was able to speak to the laird, but he shook his head and enveloped her in a hug before he let her get a word out.

"You guys are going to make me cry," Diana said once he released her. "And you sent your wife through time after me. That couldn't have been easy, my lord."

"I'd rather no' do it again," he admitted. "Stay away from druids, lass."

"I don't think that will work. We need them." Diana looked over at Cailean, who sat staring at his hands. "Master Lusk, can you join us in the map room? You need to hear my report."

The druid nodded and followed them up, but once in the map room Diana noticed that he stood back and said nothing.

"I tracked the undead from Gordon's stronghold north to a castle belonging to the Marquess of Ermindale." She marked on the wall map the approximate location of the estate. "I staked out the place, and last night I saw a bunch of nobles with an old man and two Romans at the main house. When the night sentries came out, they were all undead. The legion has taken over the estate, and they're holding some or all of the hostages there." She turned to look at Cailean. "That's what I was trying to tell you before Bhaltair shoved me into the portal."

The druid's eyes widened, and then he winced as Neac slapped him on the back of the head.

"The marquess is old," Lachlan said. "He left

court after the king ruled against him expanding his slave trade." The lord studied the wall. "He has wealth, and a vast estate, but no power or influence outside his lands. He despises the king, which has driven away what allies he had among the clans. But he kens a great deal about the most trusted nobles at court."

Raen nodded his agreement. "Once enthralled, Ermindale would tell Quintus Seneca anything he wished to ken."

"We need to take this castle," Neac said. "Now, with every warband we have."

"That's the sticky part," Diana said. "After what happened at Gordon's castle, I'd advise against going in by day. The legion has probably enthralled the entire household along with the marquess by now. At night the undead will be out in force." She tapped her finger against her lips. "Maybe if we come in from the water, and lure them away from the house, we can get some men inside, and see what's what."

"We've tried that before, and it backfired on us," Kinley said drily. "Literally, on me."

Neac shuddered. "Dinnae ask, lass," he told Diana. "'Twas horrific."

"Nor do I wish to be reminded of it," Lachlan

said and glanced at the Norseman. "How would you invade it, Tormod?"

"Red is right. No' by land." He borrowed the charcoal stick from Diana and made marks along the northern coast. "There are sea caves here that dinnae flood at high tide, and they extend back into Ermindale's lands for at least three leagues. If we take our twelve-oar birlinns, and go in by water, we might use the caves to approach the stronghold unseen."

"Why take boats when you can travel underwater?" Diana asked.

"After the battle we must transport the hostages back to their clans," Lachlan reminded her. "And we cannae risk revealing our ways to the mortals or the undead."

"Our birlinns are light," the Norseman continued. "We can carry the boats into the caves and conceal them from any undead patrols. We wait until sunrise, when the legion sleeps, and enter the castle and rescue the mortals."

"You're assuming these caves open up at the other end," Kinley put in. "And they're not filled with sleeping undead."

"They do open at the stronghold," Cailean said. When everyone turned around, he stepped forward and tapped a spot by Ermindale's castle. "There was a druid work settlement here with access to the sea caves to the north of the estate. They reported that the marquess has been using his caves to bring in more slaves."

Diana suddenly recalled what the village boy had told her. "Cailean, a kid told me that all the druids in that settlement were killed. Did you hear anything about that?"

"They disincarnated. They ended their own lives. 'Twas done to avoid capture." He fiddled with the belt of his robe. "We suspected the undead were the cause, but I wasnae permitted to tell you."

Kinley gave him a horrified look. "Cailean, we needed to know that."

"Yet you waited to tell us 'til now," Tormod drawled. "What reason for that, Ovate? Is there another sacred grove near Ermindale? Shall Red be pushed into that one while she's trying to help us save these poor mortals?" His voice rose to a shout. "What traps will you lay for her this time, when you should be fighting the facking undead with us?"

Lachlan regarded the white-faced druid. "The Viking is loud, but he speaks for the clan, and his laird. I think you should leave now, Ovate."

"I willnae betray you again, Mistress Burke. 'Twas wrong of me and my master, and I regret it still." Cailean bowed to Diana. "My lord, by your leave I will tell the conclave myself. I will tell them what the lieutenant discovered, and convince them to rule again in her favor. Until I do, I willnae return to Dun Aran." He bowed to Lachlan and Kinley before he left.

"Then mayhap you will live a little longer," Tormod called after Cailean. "Facking magic folk. We should feed them to the undead. Mayhap their treacherous blood would poison the bastarts, and we'd be rid of both."

"Stop thinking up new ways to kill the druids," Kinley said. "There's still a lot of ifs on the table. Do you really think these sea caves can be used to get at the stronghold?"

Lachlan nodded. "Ermindale would enjoy flouting the king's ruling, but he wouldnae wish to be caught at it."

"Underground passages can be used for more than the transport of slaves," Raen said. "You already said it, my lady. 'Tis the sort of place that would make a fine new lair for the legion."

"What cover can we use to approach the main house?" Neac asked Diana.

"Not much at the front or the sides, but the gardens in the back are overgrown," she told him. "I didn't see sentries posted around them, either."

For a moment there was silence and all eyes looked to Lachlan.

He nodded. "We go tonight."

"How many warbands for the attack?" Neac asked. "And who stays behind to man the castle?"

As Lachlan, Neac, and Kinley discussed that, Raen drew Diana to one side. "I dinnae want you to travel over water, no' after that dream I had. Please, stay here, where you'll be protected by our brothers."

"I'm not going to drown, Big Man, and I've already been to Ermindale by myself with no problems." Raen scowled fiercely and she rolled her eyes. "Okay, Bhaltair got me on the way home, but that doesn't count. I need you to have some faith in me, Raen. If I'm anything, I'm a survivor."

"Cailean may tell his master that you've returned," Raen warned her. "I dinnae trust the Ovate."

"It wasn't his idea," she said. "This is all Bhaltair. You should have seen how he looked at me before he…" Diana snapped her fingers. "Oh, hell, that's it." She hurried over to the laird. "I'm sorry to interrupt, my lord, but I'm druid kind. That means I'm descended from actual druids, right?"

"Aye," Lachlan said and frowned. "Did no one explain this to you?"

"Kind of, but it's not about me, not really," Diana assured him. "One more question: can two mortals make a druid baby?"

"No, lass," the laird said. "Druid kind are all blood kin."

Kinley translated that for her. "What he means is, at least one parent has to have druid DNA to make a druid baby. It's something to do with how they reincarnate. What's this about, anyway? You can't be pregnant." She saw the way Raen glowered at her and lifted her hands. "Hey, I'm never having a kid, either."

Diana shook her head. "I think I know why Bhaltair hates me so much." She sighed. "We need to deal with Ermindale now, but after the vampire dust settles, I'd like to talk to him."

"I'll see to it when I can, Diana," Lachlan said. "For now, Raen will assemble the warbands,

Tormod the birlinns, and Neac the weapons and supplies. Kinley and I will lead half the birlinns in from the east. Raen, you and Diana will bring the others in from the west. We'll carry the boats into the sea caves as Tormod suggests, and wait there until dawn before we move on the stronghold. Any questions?"

"Yes," Diana said and shrugged off the blanket covering her. She glanced down at the only other thing she was wearing. "I really can't go for a sail while I'm wearing just a patient gown. Can someone lend me some clothes?"

Chapter Twenty-Four

DIANA HAD NEVER gone sailing, but it felt good to stretch her muscles while rowing. The long, shallow boats the clan used for sea crossings were each propelled by large, blocky sails, twelve sets of oars and a primitive rudder located in the center rather than the rear. Tormod told Diana how he taught the clan to make their birlinns much smaller and lighter by fitting panels of birch bark and hollow reeds between the pine hull beams. That way, the craft could be lifted out of the water and carried by the men who rowed it. The variations in building materials created a camouflage effect on the outer hull, which allowed it to blend in when stowed in woods or brush.

"If our enemies cannae find our boats," he said, "they cannae burn them."

Raen had given Diana a crash course in Scottish galley rowing before he sat on the bench behind her and called to the other boat masters to set sail from the village docks.

"What happens if they spot our sails?" Diana asked as she worked the oars in the rolling back and forth pulls.

"'Twill be dark," Raen said, "but we will drop sails before we come within sight, and use oars only to reach the shore." He leaned forward to brush his lips across the nape of her neck. "Tormod has taught us all his Viking tricks."

"Aye, such as no' talking on the boat once we drop sail, so no one *hears* us approaching," the Norseman advised Diana.

Once they had reached the currents and caught the wind the boat began to pick up speed, and Tormod called out "Ease in," which meant to lift the oars and secure them.

"I didn't know we were going to get a rest," she said as she turned around to face Raen. "How long will it take us to reach the caves?"

"If the wind holds, we should be there just after nightfall." He tucked her braid under the back of one of Evander's tunics, which he had unearthed from an old trunk Seoc had kept in the stables. After leaving all of Diana's clothes at Gordon's stronghold, it had been that or wrapping her in his tartan again. "'Tis strange that I never realized you have the build of a Talorc. They are all tall and slender and very devious. The best of fighters among the Pritani."

"Were they also the best traitors and drunks?" As soon as she said that she regretted it. "I'm sorry, that was uncalled for."

He moved his broad shoulders. "Our tribes were enemies. What I was told of them was likely said in malice."

She laced her fingers through his. "What about your tribe? What were the Abers famous for being?"

"Big," he said flatly. "Abers always served as bodyguards for every Pritani ruler since the first because we were stronger and faster than other tribes. Some believed us too large and stupit to be suited to any other work. They didnae ken that bodyguards must always be with their rulers. My tribe were served the same foods, dressed in fine clothes, and enjoyed all the royal entertainments. Sometimes still I miss the days of my mortal life.

We Abers might never have been kings, but we lived like them."

"I know what you mean," Diana said as she looked out over the empty, dark blue waters around them, and thought of the city's busy harbor. "I'm going to miss San Diego. Not the hospital, or my brain tumor, but the city itself. It can be frantic and modern one minute, and then charming and historic the next. So many different kinds of people, too, all living together by the sea. And then there's my work. The cop who helped save my life always told me that if you save one person, you save the world."

"He was very wise," Raen said, and cupped her nape with his hand. "We wouldnae have ken about Ermindale if we hadnae saved you. And my world would never have been the same without you."

Diana would have kissed him, but Tormod called out, "Ready oars," to get them to start rowing again.

They alternated rowing with sailing when the winds permitted it, and by the time the stars came out the Norseman dropped their sails and lit a torch to signal the other boats to do the same before quickly extinguishing the flames. They rowed inland from there, and when they reached the shallows they lifted their oars and glided in with the night waves.

The shoreline appeared very rocky and completely deserted, but they waited just on the edge of the water for Lachlan and Kinley's birlinns, which arrived a short time later.

"I don't see any trails here or around the caves," Diana reported to the laird. "The undead haven't been using the beach, either."

"Take men and scout the caves to be sure," the laird told Tormod and Raen in a low voice. "If you find the undead, lure them outside to us."

While the caves were being searched, Diana and Kinley helped unload the weapons and supplies from the boats to make them easier to carry in. The laird's wife handed her a heavy velvet bag.

"This is for you," Kinley said.

Diana opened the bag and took out her Glock and the extra clip.

"Thanks, I still feel naked without it. Any druids around?"

"Oh, you're hilarious," the other woman told her. "If you so much as breathe on another druid,

I'm throwing you in the dungeon for a month. I can do that now that you're clan."

Diana noticed that Kinley didn't take any weapons for herself, but handed them off to the highlanders.

"Shouldn't you be armed, too, Captain?"

"I am, Lieutenant," she replied. She glanced at the cave entrance. "Here they are. Come on."

They walked up the shore to meet Raen, Tormod and their search party as they emerged from the caves to report to Lachlan. Diana listened to the good news and the bad, which was that while they had found all of the caves empty, the far end of the passage in the largest cave had been blocked off by tons of rock and earth.

"We were able to emerge from the others near the castle," Raen said. "But the passages and openings are narrow. Only two men may pass through them at one time."

"We'll spend the night in the largest, and use the others at daybreak," Lachlan said. "Have the lads carry the boats in now."

Diana started to follow the men inside, and then saw Neac handing Kinley unlit torches.

"Do you need a fire steel? Tormod has one."

She gasped as Kinley's hand became engulfed in white-blue flame.

"Told you I was armed," the laird's wife said as she touched her fiery hand to the torches. A moment later the flames vanished, and her hand looked completely normal. "I don't use it very often, but it's my druid talent. By the way, you don't want to get between me and the undead when I make like a flame-thrower, because you'll go..." She made a combusting sound and tossed up her hands.

"Got it. And just so you know, I am never pissing you off again."

Once they had stowed the birlinns inside the caves, the men settled in for the night, covering themselves with their tartans but keeping their long swords at hand. Lachlan made a bed for Kinley on one of the boats, but when he offered to do the same for Diana, Raen shook his head.

"Diana and I will take the first watch." He rested his war hammer on his shoulder. "She can see the trail of anyone who approaches long before they arrive."

"As you say, then, but return in two hours," the laird said. "We will want you both rested at dawn."

"There aren't any trails out here," Diana said as soon as they left the cave, and then saw his attention was elsewhere. "What's wrong?"

Raen returned and gestured for her to come down. "There is something odd at the cliffs."

Diana followed him down to the water, where he pointed to an enormous dark mound sloped down from a towering cliff to the rocky edge of the sea.

"It looks as if the cliff collapsed," he said.

"The high tides probably eroded the base, and the weight brought the rest of it down. See that one in front of it, with all the jagged rocks at the bottom? That one will be the next to go." As the wind picked up she shook out her tartan and wrapped it around her head and shoulders. "Do you want to get a closer look?"

He peered at the rockslide and nodded. "There is a path over there leading up to the cliffs. We should check for undead patrols, too."

Diana walked with him toward the cliff path, but as they drew closer to the collapsed cliff the shore became littered with broken rocks and heaps of dark soil. The debris stretched all the way to the mound, which she could now see was a small mountain of the same material, as if someone had been dumping it off the cliff for so long or so frequently it had formed a slope. She bent down to pick up a chunk of rock that bore odd striations on it. It looked as if it had been repeatedly struck by a metal tool.

"I think the undead are digging tunnels under the castle," Raen said. "'Twould explain the mound. They are filling barrows and carts with what they remove and emptying them over the cliff."

"We need to go up top and confirm that," she told Raen, who glanced back at the caves. "I'll see their trails on the cliff. Those will lead back to where they're digging. We'll have a quick look, and then we'll report what we find to the laird."

His mouth tightened. "Agreed."

The cliff path proved to be steep, and they had to go slowly to keep from sliding back down to the shore. Once Diana could see over the edge she made a long, slow scan of the empty plateau.

"What do you see?" Raen asked as he supported her from behind.

She climbed over the edge and stood on the cliff, which was glowing dull red with hundreds of crisscrossed trails.

"Legion. Lots of legion." The trails didn't

appear to be originating at the castle in the distance, but moved parallel to the shore and then disappeared into a heavily-wooded area where several huge trees had been toppled. She pointed to it. "They're hauling this stuff from over there."

Raen looked from the trees to the shore. "This willnae be quick."

"Then we'll run." When he nodded, she took off.

The big man paced her easily. When they made it to the trees they stopped and peered through them. Raen took her hand and guided her into the forest. Diana didn't hear anything but the wind and the sea at first, and then a faint hammering sound drifted to her. The deeper they went, the darker the woods became. Then they crossed a crude path lined by uprooted trees and spilled piles of rock and soil.

Raen touched his finger to her lips, and led her closer to the source of the sound. Without warning he seized her, clamping a hand over her mouth as he took cover behind some bedraggled bushes. Diana watched as a bare-chested Roman trudged past them. He led a horse hitched to a cart filled with earth, and they were headed toward the cliffs.

Once the undead had moved out of sight, Raen released her and signaled to follow him. He moved away from the path and up the side of a small hill.

Diana looked down to see torches blazing around a pit in the ground so wide and deep it could have comfortably accommodated Dun Aran and a small village. Inside it hundreds of undead were working, some mounding debris in big barrels that were pulled up by ropes. Others hammered on a wall of collapsed rock that filled one side of the pit. More of the legion were erecting elaborate frames of wood against the other three stone walls, as if they were building rooms.

Raen put his mouth right next to her ear, and murmured, "Look at the sea."

When Diana turned her head she saw the ocean, much closer than she'd thought it would be. From their position in relation to the shore, they were standing directly over the sea caves. She glanced back at the pit, and saw one of the undead diggers wrench out a huge rock from the wall. He pushed it out of the way before working on the hole it had left in the collapsed section.

A cold chill filled Diana's stomach. The

undead were digging their way into the caves. She checked the sea again and clenched her jaw. Somewhere below them, the clan lay hidden. But judging by the legion's progress, they could break through any minute. Before she could turn to Raen, lightning began to flash in the sky over them. When she looked at him, his cheek shimmered with power.

"Go back," he whispered, and kissed her temple as he held her tightly. "Tell the laird. Save the clan."

Diana tried to stop him, but her lover bolted away, ran to the edge of the pit, and jumped inside. She froze as she watched her savage man ply his war hammer against the undead. All of the Romans stopped working and rushed toward Raen, hefting their own hammers and tools as they attacked. The inside of the pit became cloudy with the ashen remains of the slain undead, but through it Diana could see her highlander fighting off the hordes lunging at him. The attacking men clawed at his tartan and tunic until they hung in shreds around his slashed arms and gouged chest. His head snapped to one side as he took a hard blow from a sledge.

Raen was the strongest, fastest, most fearless

warrior among the McDonnel Clan, but not even he could stop hundreds of undead from tearing him to pieces.

But she could.

Her legs felt good, Diana thought as she stepped out from the trees. Her knees didn't wobble, and the cut on her foot had healed. Coming back through the portal had erased all the side effects from the seizures and the stroke. She would never be stronger than she was now.

She followed the path to the edge of the pit, where she let her tartan drop and pulled off her tunic. The undead were now piling on top of Raen, wrenching his hammer from his fist and dragging him to the ground. It tore at her to see him struggling, and strengthened her resolve.

As Diana stepped out of her trousers, she flexed her legs. They felt very good, maybe even better than when she'd been in college. She'd never been much of a sprinter, but she could run a mile in just under six minutes.

She'd have to do better than that now.

Standing in only her panties, bra and boots, Diana took her dagger and hissed with pain as she sliced open her forearm from elbow to wrist. Why did people kill themselves this way? She grimaced as she dropped the blade. It really hurt.

The moment her blood began to spill off the sides of her arm the fighting in the pit came to an abrupt halt. The undead backed away from her lover as they stared at her, their eyes glittering with hunger.

"Diana," Raen gasped, and coughed.

"*You* tell the laird," she called down to him. "I'm going for a run." She raised her weapon and emptied her clip into the Romans around Raen, turning them to dust. "Anyone want some mortal?" she called out and flung the blood streaming from her wound onto the faces of the undead. "Come and get it."

Diana turned and ran, dodging trees and brush as she fled through the forest. Already her heart was bouncing against the inside of her breast like a rabbit. She could sense the hundreds of undead coming after her now, and then heard the sounds of snarling and snapping behind her. For this to work she couldn't get there too fast, so she slowed her pace to give the front runners a little time to catch up. Branches snapped and leaves thrashed all around her as the undead began appearing.

Okay, now she had to be faster.

Pouring on the speed made her thighs burn, and her bleeding arm throbbed like a root canal gone wrong. Still, the pain was a lot less than she'd expected. She'd gone through all the levels of hell during her tumor treatment: puking until she passed out, watching handfuls of her hair fall into the sink every morning, hiding her baldness with itchy wigs that made her sweat. One night she'd even sat and nibbled on imaginary French fries while she listened to a hallucination of Tonio singing the Ave Maria. Then she'd cried so hard her eyes had swollen shut. A cut on her arm and some strained muscles were nothing.

Her heart didn't hurt a bit, but that was because she was saving his. She only wished she had told him she loved him, but Raen already knew that.

I think I'm falling in love with you.

I'll catch you with my heart when you do.

A cold hand clawed at her back, as if to remind her she was supposed to be faster than this, but she focused on the cliff path. It was only a hundred yards away now, so she used every bit of energy she had left to sprint for it. The undead were almost on top of her, and if they dragged her to the ground all this would be for nothing. She was better than that—better than them.

Just before she reached the cliff path Diana swerved and took a running dive. She soared out over the edge of the cliff as if she had wings. That lovely moment lasted all of a blink before she plummeted downward. She rolled over in mid-air to see the hundreds of ravenous, mindless undead jumping over the edge after her. They shrieked as they saw the jagged rocks waiting for them below.

Raen would live, Diana thought a moment before she slammed into the endless brick wall of the sea, and Tonio had been right. She had saved the one man she had ever loved. Since he was her world, that was safe, too. That she had to die to do it didn't bother her in the least.

Chapter Twenty-Five

❧

QUINTUS SENECA WATCHED from the balcony as the last of the guards caught the blood scent on the air, dropped their weapons and ran off. He didn't know what had caused the frenzy, but it had effectively emptied the stronghold and the grounds of the starving undead. Behind him his new prefect hovered anxiously, too well-fed to join the hordes of men streaming toward the cliffs, but nervous for other reasons. Like them, all of his plans would soon be nothing but ash.

"How many have we lost?" he finally asked without looking at Ficini.

"All of the miners, the guards, the sentries and the mortals we just turned," the prefect said. "The raiding party remains intact, but they are not enough to stand against the McDonnels. Tribune, the clan will be coming for the hostages, and they are no longer enthralled. We should kill them and flee."

"Dinnae lose heart, Quintus," the Marquess of Ermindale said as he came to join him. "We will go to join up with the reserves in the lowlands. There we will make more troops, and train them, and plan for the next opportunity. As for the hostages, they may be taken and enthralled again when we are ready to move against the king."

He turned to regard the undead noble. "Do you imagine yourself my commander, simply because I turned you?"

"No, Quintus," Ermindale said with a smile. "I am but the man who fed every member of his family to you, including my youngest daughter, whom you facked before you ended her. Ah, yes, I watched through the spy hole to your bed chamber. Then I gave you my life by allowing you to drain most of my blood from my body, and my soul by drinking your blood, and becoming undead. So now I am ready to be more." He turned and drove his dagger into Ficini's chest.

The prefect tottered backward and collapsed into a pile of dust. "I am your new second."

Quintus drew his sword and held it at the noble's scrawny throat. "You dare murder one of mine."

"I am yours," the old man reminded him. "And I am far more valuable to you than that fool ever was. I own a dozen estates in the south that I use to house slaves before I sell them. We will occupy and modify them for our needs and purposes. The slaves will make excellent soldiers after you turn them, and no one will ken where we are." The old man looked down the length of the steel. "You forget that I also possess the only manner in which you will leave here alive, Tribune. Kill me, and you kill yourself."

Slowly Quintus lowered his sword, and looked down at the pile of ash. From it he retrieved his red cloak, but did not bother to shake it clean before he draped it over the marquess's narrow shoulders.

"Very well, Prefect. We shall go south."

"As you command, Tribune." The marquess bowed. "And please, call me Dougal."

Chapter Twenty-Six

THE CRACKLE OF fire licked at Raen's ears, while the smell of wood smoke filled his head. When the taste of whiskey seeped into his mouth, he swallowed it reflexively. More followed, too much and too quickly, and he choked. His muscles bunched with pain as he pushed himself up to see Neac taking a drink from the bottle in his hand before he nodded to someone.

"I thought Abers indestructible," the chieftain said as he plied a damp rag over Raen's mouth. "And yet it required only two hundred of the blood-suckling bastarts to take you down. Lad, I'm ashamed of you."

Lachlan eased down beside him and draped him with his own tartan. "How do you feel?"

"Hurt." The word rasped from his mouth as he looked at the other, solemn faces around them. He touched his battered face as he remembered jumping into the pit. "Legion?"

"Slain," the laird said but looked sick now. "'Twas Diana, lad. We came out of the cave when the rock began to shift, and saw her jump from the cliffs. The undead followed."

"They followed her blood trail, and came from all directions," Neac added. "The woods, the village, the castle, hundreds of them. They all went over, even when the sun rose and they were burning as they jumped–"

"That's enough," a white-faced Kinley said as she sat down on the other side of him, and took hold of his broken hand. "Hey," she said to him. "You are in so much trouble. As soon as you're better, I'm going to make you clean out all the privies at the castle. Twice."

Raen remembered now. His brave, beautiful lass, standing in her little bits of black lace, telling him she was going for a run. Painfully, he managed to sit up. They were on the beach with the birlenns, and a fire was burning. He looked up the cliff.

"She cut herself to make them chase her," he

said. "To save the clan." He closed his eyes. "To save me."

"We found the tunnels they were digging from the stronghold," Lachlan said. "They must have caused the cave-in that sealed off the sea cave."

It took three tries before Raen was able to stand, but once he was steady enough he hobbled to the edge of the sea.

Tormod joined him there, his clothes dripping wet. "I went in after her, but I couldnae find her," he said, his voice hoarse with pain. "I'll go again."

"No," Raen said.

His nightmare had come true. His Diana was somewhere out there, waiting for him. He waded in, ignoring the sting of the salt water in his wounds, but stopped when the laird caught up with him.

"Permit me the honor," Lachlan said. "She will have a clan burial, but you are too badly wounded, lad."

"I will find her body," Raen told him, and looked in his laird's eyes, stopping him. "I must do this."

With that he sank under the water, and swam toward the depths.

◈

LACHLAN GAZED out at the moonlit waves, silvery and cold. As he waited, he felt Kinley come to his side.

"He'll come back, won't he?" Kinley asked as she stared out at the sea. She didn't seem to be aware of the tears sliding down her cheeks. "He has to. We can't lose both of them."

"I dinnae ken if he can heal from this," Lachlan said and put his arm around his wife's shoulders. "Even if he comes back, he willnae be the same." He glanced over her head at Tormod, who looked as if he might go after Raen. "No, Viking. We must honor his wishes."

Neac joined them, and in a low voice said, "The last of the hostages have been recovered, and the castle searched. The undead and the marquess are gone." He nodded toward the other end of the shore. "And the magic folk are here."

Lachlan looked over to see Bhaltair and Cailean leading hundreds of druids out of the sea caves toward them. He released his wife.

"Tormod, gather the men. Kinley, go into the cave and see that the nobles are ready to travel."

"Nice try," she said and didn't move. "Let me talk to Bhaltair. I don't want to use his head as a soccer ball. Much."

"Nor do I," he told her gently. "But your hands are on fire, love, and I think you may burn off his face."

"Oh, facking hell." She shook out the flames and folded her arms around her waist. "Tormod, come on. Let's gather the damn men."

Lachlan went with Neac to intercept the druids, Bhaltair in front.

"Diana Burke is dead," Lachlan said flatly. "You are not wanted here."

"Leave us in peace to mourn our sister," Neac added.

The old druid tucked his hands into his sleeves. "We come to pay our respects. She was our sister, too."

Neac stepped up to Bhaltair, thrusting his face close. "You've no respect for anything but your own scrawny arse. Be gone with you, before I forget that you're a facking weak, useless old man, and–"

Light burst between them, and Neac went hurtling backward to land with a splash in the water. He surfaced, spluttering, and stared aghast at the old druid.

"Have you gone daft?" Lachlan demanded of the old man, and then watched in disbelief as Bhaltair and his people walked straight past him.

The McDonnels made way for the druids, their expressions filled with contempt. Bhaltair ignored them as he went to the edge of the water, and stood until all the others had formed a line on either side of him. They stood and watched as Raen emerged, Diana's limp body in his arms, and began wading toward them.

Though at first anger flashed across his haggard face, grim determination replaced it as he made directly for Bhaltair.

"Save her," the big man said, falling to his knees in the surf. "Give her my life. Cast her death on me."

The other druids turned to Bhaltair and waited for him to reply.

"The gods sent Diana Burke to us," the old druid said. "She was to be one of us, and one of the clan. In my pride I didnae see it. I spoke against her, and I forced her to leave. Tonight we saw her as she went willingly to her death, that this clansman and the McDonnels might live."

"No," Kinley said to Lachlan. "Don't let them make Raen undead. Diana wouldn't have wanted that."

There were murmurs from the warriors all around.

"We'll make no more undead," Cailean said, raising a hand for silence. He turned to Bhaltair. "Master?"

The old druid nodded solemnly and turned his grim face toward Raen.

"Will you share your life with her, Tharaen Aber, and help us heal her?" Bhaltair asked.

Raen looked down at Diana's pale face. "Yes."

As Bhaltair murmured the words of an ancient spell, all of the druids did the same. They bowed down and placed their hands in the water, and Lachlan felt their power saturate the air. The sea before them filled with golden light, growing brighter as it encircled and then engulfed Raen and Diana.

"Oh, my god," Kinley whispered as Raen's battered face began to heal, and the wound on Diana's arm sealed itself. "Oh, Lachlan."

Brilliant light like the brightest stars danced along their skins. As it flared Diana coughed and sputtered, and her eyes slowly opened.

Raen gaped down at her, smiling past the tears that brimmed in his wide eyes. Then he hugged her fiercely as the teardrops began to fall.

As Kinley quietly wept, Lachlan held her to his side.

"Tharaen Aber and Diana McDonnel," Bhaltair intoned. "Now you are two souls made one, and you shall never die."

৩৬৩

As FOAMY WAVES SPLASHED around them, Diana watched the last of Raen's wounds heal. "What happened?"

"What didnae?" he said with a laugh. He gently set her on her feet and brushed her wet hair back from her face. "I nearly died in the pit, and then you made yourself bait and lured the undead away. Lachlan told me you threw yourself off a cliff into the sea, and all the undead followed, you reckless wench."

"But it worked," she said, grinning. "I saved you, you saved me, and now I'm immortal. Good thing the druids showed up."

"Aye." He rubbed a hand over his face. "But

the druids didnae raise you from the dead as they did Kinley. They shared my immortal soul with you. I will have to be nice to them now. Come here."

She laughed as she launched herself at him, encircling his neck with her arms as she kissed him with all the joy and love flooding through her.

"You know what this means," she said, touching her brow to his. "You're really stuck with me. We can never break up because I'll always be around, forever. You sure you're up for that?"

"Well, if it doesnae work with us, there is always Tormod," he said. "I find him handsome, in the Viking way, and you have seen how he cannae conceal his passion for me." He laughed as she thumped on his chest. "Now I have made you jealous. Good. Now come." He scooped her up in his strong arms. "Our clan awaits us."

Raen carried her out of the waves onto the shore, where he set her down to clasp arms with their clansmen. Tormod stalked over to her and shouted in his native tongue words that didn't sound like "welcome back" to Diana. Then he glanced down, tore off his cloak and covered her with it.

"I cannae beat you myself," the Viking said, "but I will persuade Aber to do so. Regularly if you cannae remember your clothes. And I will watch."

Diana found herself being hugged until her ribs nearly cracked, and then chuckled as the Norseman stalked off. To Raen she said, "He might be more into me, actually." As Cailean came to join them she felt like slapping him, but instead forced a smile before she asked Raen, "Is everyone okay? Any casualties?"

"Naught but us, lass." He reached up to touch her cheek, which tingled oddly, and then he regarded the young druid. "You did this for her, but it saved me as well. Thank you."

Cailean shook his head. "'Twas no' my doing, Seneschal. Master Flen brought the others here after I spoke for Diana." He glanced over at the old druid, who was talking with Lachlan. "Only a master as wise as he can perform such magic." To Diana he said, "I am glad you are returned to us, Lieutenant."

"Me, too," she said as she surveyed her lover. "You look better than the last time I saw you." She rubbed at her tingling face, and then felt the tiny striations on her skin. "Uh-oh. Is this what I think it is?"

"You've been marked again," Raen said and showed her the jag of ink on her other palm, that now marked either side of the long, thin scar that stretched from her elbow to wrist. It continued up and over her shoulder and onto her neck and face. "We share a soul now, so my spirit has claimed you for itself."

"We match," Diana said, tracing the ink and smiling as she felt it move under her finger tips. "Boy, are you in trouble the minute we're alone."

The big man caught her face between his hands, and kissed her as the other McDonnels cheered them on. When he lifted his head he said, "Thank you for my life. I love you. And if you ever do that again, I am chaining you to my bed for the rest of eternity."

She eyed the cliffs. "It would definitely be worth it." Seeing who was approaching them, she drew back. "I need to talk to Bhaltair —alone. Okay?"

Raen gave the old druid a hard look, but nodded and walked up to join the clan.

"Mistress McDonnel," Bhaltair said and

bowed to her. "I am happy you are come back to us."

"You are the unhappiest guy in Scotland right now, Master Flen, and it's because of these." She tapped the corner of her eye. "The woman you loved had the same color eyes. Cailean told me. She left you for a mortal who got her pregnant, right?"

Bhaltair stiffened. "'Twas a long time ago, and it doesnae have anything to do with you. Please refrain from meddling, Mistress. You are clan now."

"I'm kind of a meddler, and I'm also druid. My eye color is very rare, even in my time, so it's also possible that I'm your first love's descendent." Diana leaned closer. "And if I am, that means I'm yours, too. The laird told me that two mortals can't have a druid baby. If that woman is my ancestor, then *you* were the father of her child."

"Aye," he finally said, and instead of seeming shocked he gave her a sad smile. "You are my blood. The first moment I saw you, I felt it, and then realized what Yana had done."

Diana felt a little taken aback. "Why didn't you say anything to me?"

"What could I have told you? That she took

my child from me, and raised it as his? That it broke my heart so badly that I never wed or had children in any of my other incarnations?" He cleared his throat. "That was why I wished you gone. I couldnae bear to look upon you. You are every reason that I am a fool."

"Why? She did this, not you." When he hung his head she said, "Look, if I'm your blood, then you're mine. You're my family, Master Flen. I've never had that, and I want you to be a part of this new life you've given me." Diana smiled a little. "Would it help if I call you Grandpa?"

"Gods save me, no," he said quickly. He took her hand and brought her knuckles to his lips. "I will be friend and kin to you, Diana, and if you are ever in need of a proud and silly old man, then I am yours to command."

He walked with her up to where Raen was waiting, and handed her off to him with a stern look.

"You should ken that Diana is my blood kin, Seneschal. I willnae see her dishonored by a man who enjoys her affections, but doesnae have the right to them." As they both stared at him he smiled primly. "You will wed her as soon as can be arranged, or I shall find another pit of undead, and push you in it myself."

The big man grinned. "Aye, sir."

"Don't I get a say in this?' Diana asked, and held up her hands as both men glowered at her. "Okay, yes, I'll marry him." She went into her lover's arms, and sighed with delight against his chest. "Let's go home."

Chapter Twenty-Seven

❧

SEVEN DAYS LATER Cailean sat in a corner of the great hall at Dun Aran and watched the hungry clansmen attack the platters of food that Meg Talley and her maids had set out for the wedding feast. Neac manned the taps of the whiskey and ale bottles, while Tormod was demonstrating a Viking dance that entailed a great deal of jumping, chest-pounding, and snatching off the caps of the maids and tossing them in the air.

In the center of it all stood Diana and Raen, dressed in fine clothes, their faces bright with their sparkling skinwork, and their love for each other.

Bhaltair came and handed him a tankard of ale before he sat down beside him. "She is returned, and saved, and wed. She even claims me as blood kin, which is probably unwise, given how stupit I have been, but I am proud to call her mine." He waited, and when Cailean did not reply he said, "All has been mended, Ovate Lusk. You must speak to me now, or take for yourself another master."

"Kinley is mine," Cailean said. When he felt his master stiffen, he smiled. "No' my lover. My blood kin. I've ken it since the night we resurrected her in the grove. I felt her soul return from the loch of stars."

The old druid gave him a sharp look. "But you told me that you havenae sired any bairns."

"I was with the countess when her family died of plague," Cailean said calmly. "Her match to Gordon was done quickly to provide for the two clans. When I left I didnae ken she was already carrying a child." He met his master's gaze. "The son she will bear is mine."

"Kinley and Diana have naught to do with our plan," Bhaltair protested.

"These women crossing over, they are not come to us by chance." Cailean looked at the laird's wife, and felt again the tug of their kinship.

"I think them part of the Great Design, a part we didnae plan."

Bhaltair made a gesture for silence as one of the clansmen passed in front of them. "You will have to go before the conclave about this. The farseers must be consulted."

"When we return, I shall," Cailean said and nodded at the women. "What about them?"

"Two are not enough to prove anything," the old druid said. "If more come, then we will revisit the notion. But let us not debate this today, lad. Today we celebrate a wrong made right, and a love that will endure."

"You, speaking of love," Cailean mused as he eyed his tankard. "How much whiskey have they given you?"

"No' enough," Bhaltair said as he gazed fondly at Diana. "I think she has my nose from my first incarnation. And mayhap my shoulders. I had good, strong shoulders in that life, you know."

"Aye," Cailean replied and took a drink and sighed. "And we will need them when the next of our daughters arrives."

THE END

• • • • •

Another Immortal Highlander awaits you in
Evander (Immortal Highlander Book 3).

For a sneak peek, turn the page.

Sneak Peek

Evander (Immortal Highlander Book 3)

Excerpt

Rachel Ingram walked out onto the garden balcony overlooking the swimming pavilion, where her father's infinity pool spread like a lake suspended in the air. Beyond it his beloved red gum eucalyptus trees climbed the curves of the estate's rolling green hills. They provided an illusion of privacy, as if all the world belonged to Avalon. Sometimes, looking out at the pristine grounds beneath the porcelain blue sky, it seemed as if it did.

In Rancho Santa Fe, one of America's wealth-

iest towns, all of the residents wanted that illusion.
In the Covenant, the most exclusive neighbor-
hood within its boundaries, they got it.

A hundred acres beyond the Ingrams' trea-
sured old trees and high, sculpted hedges lay other
immense estate houses belonging to their billion-
aire neighbors. No one went to the tech mogul's
smart mansion to ask for a spare charger, or to the
self-help guru's opulent villa to borrow a cup of
sugar. That was simply not done. Plenty of neighbors went to the Olympic gold medalist's gaudy
shrine to himself and his sport, but he was more
of a sociable guy.

"He's holding another party in that over-sized
frat house," Sheldon Ingram had often
complained to his wife and daughter. "I can hear
them rolling the kegs from here."

Rachel smelled the airy sweetness of her
mother's white roses, and glanced over hundreds
of blooms draping the loggia. Her parents' lounge
chairs still sat beside the old stone table that Beatrice Ingram had fallen in love with during their
European honeymoon. Her father had secretly
shipped it from Scotland to present it to his wife
on their first anniversary, along with Avalon.

A few withered petals had fallen on the

massive slab of green-streaked granite, which now looked like a toppled tombstone overgrown with moss.

The scent of a familiar, leathery cologne drifted around her as quiet footsteps approached, and she braced herself against the railing.

"Good morning, Paul."

"I'm so sorry to disturb you, Rachel." Her parents' attorney came to join her, his sober suit fitted as if he'd been born with navy silk as an outer shell. "How are you feeling?"

She wanted to tell him that she'd spent the morning throwing up, but he didn't need to hear that.

"I'm all right, I guess."

"I thought I'd stop in and see if you'd come to a decision about the estate." His smile turned slightly uneasy. "I understand how difficult this must be for you, but the buyer is hoping for an answer on their offer soon."

Difficult? Rachel frowned. Avalon had killed her parents. She had to sell it, only because no one would let her bulldoze it into the ground. But she couldn't say that to Paul Carver. Deliberately destroying a multi-million dollar mansion instead of selling it wasn't acceptable, and in a few hours Paul would be her father-in-law.

No one wanted crazy in the family.

"I can't deal with the sale today," she said. "David and I are going into the city to get married. Then we're going to drive up and spend the weekend at the beach house." She hated how dreary she sounded, talking about her wedding as if it were a dental appointment. Since the funerals she felt so exhausted and depressed, and sometimes just getting out of bed took all her strength. "I'm sorry."

"Keeping it simple is probably best," the attorney said quickly. He agreed with everything she said but, now that she had inherited the Ingram fortune, everyone except David was doing that. "Call me when you get back in town, and then we'll talk." He touched her shoulder before he retreated inside the mansion.

A few minutes later the purring sound of a Rolls came from the front of the house, and Rachel watched as the man who would be her father-in-law sped down the long curving drive, pausing only for security to open the gates.

For once Paul's behavior actually registered as odd to her. It seemed as if he couldn't get away from her and Avalon fast enough, and she wondered why. Her father had made Paul a very wealthy man, and Rachel was marrying his son. Maybe he didn't want her to, or he simply didn't like her. Yet when she'd told him they were getting married, she'd felt his relief as surely as if he'd voiced it.

Rachel had often wondered if she should tell her fiancé about her uncanny intuition. But David might think she was delusional, and over the last few weeks her sensitivity had been so muted she rarely even felt her own emotions. His father had to be happy about the marriage. If nothing else, Rachel was now one of the richest women in the country.

It was all thanks to her dad, who had used the millions he inherited from his corporate CEO father to become the most successful start-up investor in modern history. From solar-powered smart phones to 3-D printed replacement heart valves, the ventures Sheldon Ingram bankrolled always proved wildly innovative as well as profitable in the extreme.

"I'm not a genius," Sheldon told a reporter once. "I invest in people. Guessing which ones are going to change the world is what I do best."

Her father had slowed down only long enough to romance and marry Beatrice, Rachel's Italian heiress mother, who had brought old world money, blue blood, and ancient connections with European royalty as her dowry. He'd built this Mediterranean chateau for her when she'd gotten pregnant with Rachel, called it Avalon, and then set up his kingdom in the Covenant.

Her father had always fancied himself a Merlin rather than a King Arthur. Since everything he touched turned to gold, Midas might have been more appropriate. Thanks to him, Rachel would never have to work, or worry, or do anything except what she wanted.

But all she wanted was what she could never again have.

Rachel would happily give every cent she'd inherited to hear once more the reassurance of her father's deep voice, and the sweet trill of her mother's easy laughter. They had given her so much love she'd never once considered how it would feel to be without it. She would beggar herself to bring them back to life. If only she'd skipped the weekend shopping trip to L.A. with David and his mother. She'd have been here when the fire started. She knew she would have woken up in time to get them out of the house—or not.

I could have died with them.

How long Rachel stood there wishing for what she could never have, she didn't know. She only came out of her trance when her fingers began to cramp, and glanced down to see the white-knuckled grip she had on the balcony railing. Carefully she released it and turned around to face Avalon, now fully cleaned and restored. The only signs of the electrical fire that had consumed the master suite and burned her parents to death was scorched earth around the newly-built wing. In another week the landscaping company would finish putting in the new sod, and even that would be gone.

Like her parents, cremated in their own bed.

"Darling?"

From inside the sunroom David Carver emerged, his elegant hands holding two slender goblets of champagne. From his razor-cut short blond hair to his spotless white shirt and shorts he looked immaculate, but then he always did. Rachel knew he had spent the morning playing tennis at one of his mother's charity fundraisers, and yet he still appeared pressed and polished, as if he'd just gotten dressed.

Rachel admired his perfection—who didn't? —but something about his appearance this morning bothered her. He seemed almost too spotless. Did her fiancé even have the ability to sweat?

• • • • •

Buy *Evander (Immortal Highlander Book 3)* Now

DO ME A FAVOR?

You can make a big difference.

Reviews are the most powerful tools I have when it comes to getting attention for my books. Much as I'd like it, I don't have the financial muscle of a New York publisher. I can't take out full page ads in the newspaper—not yet, anyway.

But I do have something much more powerful. It's something that those publishers would kill for: **a committed and loyal group of readers.**

Honest reviews of my books help bring them to the attention of other readers. If you've enjoyed this book I would so appreciate it if you could spend a few minutes leaving a review—any length you like.

Thank you so much!

MORE BOOKS BY HH

For a complete, up-to-date book list, visit
HazelHunter.com/books.

Get notifications of new releases and special
promotions by joining my newsletter!

Glossary

Here are some brief definitions to help you navigate the medieval world of the Immortal Highlanders.

Abyssinia - ancient Ethiopia
acolyte - novice druid in training
addled - confused
advenae - Roman citizen born of freed slave parents
afterlife - what happens after death
animus attentus - Latin for "listen closely"
apotheoses - highest points in the development of something
Aquilifer - standard bearer in a Roman legion
arse - ass

auld - old

Ave - Latin for "Hail"

aye - yes

bairn - child

banger - explosion

banshee in a bannock - making a mountain out of a molehill

barrow - wheelbarrow

bastart - bastard

bat - wooden paddle used to beat fabrics while laundering

battering ram - siege device used to force open barricaded entries and other fortifications

battle madness - Post Traumatic Stress Disorder

bawbag - scrotum

Belgia - Belgium

birlinn - medieval wooden boat propelled by sails and oars

blaeberry - European fruit that resembles the American blueberry

blind - cover device

blood kin - genetic relatives

bonny - beautiful

boon - gift or favor

brambles - blackberry bushes

bran'y - brandy

Brank's bridle mask - iron muzzle in an iron
framework that enclosed the head

Britannia - Latin for "Britain"

brownie - Scottish mythical benevolent spirit that
aids in household tasks but does not wish to
be seen

buckler - shield

Caledonia - ancient Scotland

caligae - type of hobnailed boots worn by the
Roman legion

cannae - can't

cannel - cinnamon

canny - shrewd, sharp

catch-fire - secret and highly combustible Pritani
compound that can only be extinguished by sand

Centurio - Latin for "Centurions"

century - Roman legion unit of 100 men

chatelaine - woman in charge of a large house

Chieftain - second highest-ranking position within
the clan; the head of a specific Pritani tribe

choil - unsharpened section of a knife just in front
of the guard

Choosing Day - Pritani manhood ritual during
which adolescent boys are tattooed and offer
themselves to empowering spirits

chow - food

cistern - underground reservoir for storing
rain water

claymore - two-edged broadsword

clout - strike

cohort - Roman legion tactical military unit of
approximately 500 men

cold pantry - underground cache or room for the
storage of foods to be kept cool

comely - attractive

conclave - druid ruling body

conclavist - member of the druid ruling body

contubernium - squad of eight men; the smallest
Roman legion formation

COP - Command Observation Post

cosh - to bash or strike

couldnae - couldn't

counter - in the game of draughts, a checker

courses - menstrual cycle

cow - derogatory term for woman

Coz - cousin

croft - small rented farm

cudgel - wooden club

da - dad

daft - crazy

dappled - animal with darker spots on its coat

defendi altus - Latin for "defend high"

detail - military group assignment

dinnae - don't

disincarnate - commit suicide

diviner - someone who uses magic or extra sensory perception to locate things

doesnae - doesn't

dories - small boats used for ship to shore transport

draughts - board game known as checkers in America

drawers - underpants

drivel - nonsense

drover - a person who moves herd animals over long distances

dung - feces

EDC - Every Day Carry, a type of knife

excavators - tunnel-diggers

fack - fuck

facking - fucking

faodail - lucky find

fash - feel upset or worried

fathom - understand

fere spectare - Latin for "about face"

ferret out - learn

festers - becomes infected

fetters - restraints

fibula - Roman brooch or pin for fastening clothes

filching - stealing

fisher - boat

fishmonger - person who sells fish for food

floor-duster - Pritani slang for druid

foam-mouth - rabies

Francia - France

Francian - French

free traders - smugglers

frenzy - mindless, savagely aggressive, mass-attack behavior caused by starving undead smelling fresh blood

fripperies - showy or unnecessary ornament

Germania - Germany

god-ridden - possessed

Great Design - secret druid master plan

greyling - species of freshwater fish in the salmon family

gut rot - cancer of the bowel

hasnae - hasn't

heid doon arse up - battle command: head down, ass up

Hetlandensis - oldest version of the modern name Shetland

Hispania - Roman name for the Iberian peninsula (modern day Portugal and Spain)

hold - below decks, the interior of a ship

holk - type of medieval ship used on rivers and close to coastlines as a barge

hoor - whore

huddy - stupid, idiotic

impetus - Latin for "attack"

incarnation - one of the many lifetimes of a druid

isnae - isn't

jeeked - extremely tired

Joe - GI Joe shortened, slang for American soldier

jotunn - Norse mythic giantess

justness - justice

kelpie - water spirit of Scottish folklore, typically taking the form of a horse, reputed to delight in the drowning of travelers

ken - know

kirtle - one piece garment worn over a smock

kuks - testicles

lad - boy

laird - lord

lapstrake - method of boat building where the hull planks overlap

larder - pantry

lass - girl

league - distance measure of approximately three miles

Legio nota Hispania - Latin name for The Ninth Legion

loggia - open-side room or house extension that is partially exposed to the outdoors

magic folk - druids

mam - mom

mannish - having characteristics of a man

mantle - loose, cape-like cloak worn over garments

mayhap - maybe

milady - my lady

milord - my lord

missive - message

mormaer - regional or provincial ruler, second only to the Scottish king

motte - steep-sided man-made mound of soil on which a castle was built

mustnae - must not

naught - nothing

no' - not

Norrvegr - ancient Norway

Noto - Latin for "Attention"

Optia - rank created for female Roman Legion recruit Fenella Ivar

Optio - second in command of a Roman legion century

orachs - slang term for chanterelle mushrooms

orcharders - slang for orchard farmers

ovate - Celtic priest or natural philosopher

palfrey - docile horse

paludamentum - cloak or cape worn fastened at one shoulder by Romans military commanders

parati - Latin for "ready"

parched - thirsty, dry

parlay - bargain

penchants - strong habits or preferences

perry - fermented pear juice

Pict - member of an ancient people inhabiting northern Scotland in Roman times

pillion - seated behind a rider

pipes - bagpipes

pisspot - chamber pot, toilet

plumbed - explored the depth of

poppet - doll

poppy juice - opium

pottage - a thick, stew-like soup of meat and vegetables

pox-ridden - infected with syphilis

praefectus - Latin for "prefect"

Prefect - senior magistrate or governor in the ancient Roman world

Pritani - Britons (one of the people of southern Britain before or during Roman times)

privy - toilet

quim - woman's genitals

quoits - medieval game like modern ring toss

repulsus - Latin for "drive back"

rescue bird - search and rescue helicopter

roan - animal with mixed white and pigmented hairs

roo - to pluck loose wool from a sheep

rumble - fight

Sassenachs - Scottish term for English people

scunner - source of irritation or strong dislike

sea stack - column of eroded cliff or shore rock standing in the sea

Seid - Norse magic ritual

selkie - mythical creature that resembles a seal in the water but assumes human form on land

semat - undershirt

seneschal - steward or major-domo of a medieval great house

shouldnae - shouldn't

shroud - cloth used to wrap a corpse before burial

skelp - strike, slap, or smack

skin work - tattoos

smalls - men's underwear

SoCal - slang for southern California

solar - rooms in a medieval castle that served as
the family's private living and sleeping quarters

spellfire - magically-created flame

spellmark - visible trace left behind by the use
of magic

spew - vomit

spindle - wooden rod used in spinning

squared - made right

stad - Scots Gaelic for "halt"

staunch weed - yarrow

stupit - stupid

Svitiod - ancient Sweden

swain - young lover or suitor

swived - have sexual intercourse with

taobh - Scots Gaelic for "Flank"

tempest - storm

tester - canopy over a bed

the pox - smallpox

thickhead - dense person

thimblerig - shell game

thrawn - stubborn

'tis - it is

'tisnt - it isn't

toadies - lackeys

tonsure - shaved crown of the head

TP - toilet paper

traills - slaves

trencher - wooden platter for food

trews - trousers

trials - troubles

Tribune - Roman legionary officer

tuffet - low seat or footstool

'twas - it was

'twere - it was

'twill - it will

'twould - it would

Vesta - Roman goddess of the hearth

wand-waver - Pritani slang for druid

warband - group of warriors sent together on a specific mission

wasnae - wasn't

wee - small

wench - girl or young woman

wenching - womanizing or chasing women for the purposes of seduction

white plague - tuberculosis

whoreson - insult; the son of a prostitute

widdershins - in a direction contrary to the sun's course, considered as unlucky; counterclockwise.

willnae - will not

woad - plant with leaves that produce blue dye

wouldnae - would not

ye - you

yer - your

Pronunciation Guide

A selection of the more challenging words in the Immortal Highlander series.

Bhaltair Flen - BAHL-ter Flen
Black Cuillin - COO-lin
Cailean Lusk - KAH-len Luhsk
Dun Aran - doon AIR-uhn
Evander Talorc - ee-VAN-der TAY-lork
faodail - FOOT-ill
Fiona Marphee - fee-O-nah MAR-fee
Lachlan McDonnel - LOCK-lin mik-DAH-nuhl
Loch Sìorraidh - Lock SEEO-rih
Neacal Uthar - NIK-ul OO-thar
Seoc Talorc - SHOK TAY-lork
Tharaen Aber - theh-RAIN AY-burr
Tormod Liefson - TORE-mod LEEF-sun

Dedication

For Mr. H.

Copyright

Making Magic

❦

Welcome to Making Magic, a little section at the end of the book where I can give readers a glimpse at what I do. It's not edited and my launch team doesn't read it because it's kind of a last minute thing. Therefore typos will surely follow. Be careful where you step.

I think I write about Scotland because of the weather.

I've lived in California all my life. Sure, there are some rainy and cool spots in the northern part of the state. But here in SoCal, it's pretty sunny and not often chilly. But in my writer's head, a cool, rainy day is the perfect time for reading and for writing. On the rare occasion that it does rain here, I'll actually just watch it for a while before I write. It provides a kind of white noise that's both soothing and keeps distractions at bay. It's perfect!

Of course I don't have to drive in it much, since I no longer have an epic commute. You'd think from all the accidents that happen on a rainy day here that we Angelenos don't know how to drive in the rain (which may be true in my case!). But the reality is that oil from our millions of cars builds up on the roadways. When the first rain finally hits, it's slicker than owl snot.

Which is all to say that I think I'd like the weather in the medieval Scottish highlands. I don't think I'd want to live in the 14th century, but I'll take a double helping of rain by the bucket, lightning over a wind-whipped sea, and clouds so dark that it feels like night.

Thank you for reading, thank you for reviewing, and I'll see you between the covers soon.

XOXO,

HH

Los Angeles, September 2017

Read Me

Like Me

Grab My Next Book?